The Camelot Puzzle

Book One of *The Marbles Saga*

Steve Peaslee

Chapter One

The Visitor

JoJo Mallory knew something wasn't right even before she opened her eyes. Sitting up in her bed, she pulled her tangled mop of auburn hair out of her face and stared at the bed across the room. Straining to focus, it took a couple of seconds to remember that it wasn't her little sister sleeping soundly under the covers, but rather JoJo's best friend, Marcy DiPietro.

"Hello."

JoJo screamed. This, of course, caused Marcy to shoot into a suddenly-awake, fully upright position. Then, she screamed, too.

Standing just inside the room, and about five feet from the end of either bed, was the shortest man either girl had ever seen. With a beard. And a jacket and funny hat. If his greeting had been intended to break the ice, he succeeded.

"Who *are* you?" JoJo demanded, pulling the blanket up to her chest protectively. "And what are you doing in here? *Dad!*"

"He is not here," the little man said, almost sadly. For such a small person he had a deep rich voice, the kind you would normally associate with a much larger man, like a professional football player.

JoJo stared at him, the words hitting her like a sledgehammer. *He is not here?* She felt more than capable of taking care of herself in most situations, including playing pond hockey with the boys, but this was different. Completely different. This was a strange man in her bedroom, for crying out loud!

"Dad!" she tried again. They lived on the first floor of a three-story house, and her father's bedroom wasn't all that far from hers. If he was there, he could hear her, no doubt about it. "*Dad!*"

"Dad! *Mister Mallory!*" Marcy joined in, her voice a few pitches higher than JoJo's, but just as frantic.

The little man stood patiently and waited, his hands folded in front of him, on his face a look of resignation. He never once looked back over his shoulder as if someone might be entering the room behind him. He knew there was no one else in the house.

Indeed, the other three Mallory girls had all spent the night at the houses of their friends, although JoJo was certain that the two high schoolers had gone to parties that their father would not have approved of, had he known. Her little sister, Scrap, was only eight years old, and was staying with her best friend for the entire weekend. That had all led to Marcy – whose real name was Marcella – eating pizza and spending the night here with JoJo.

The last they'd heard from JoJo's father was when he wished them one final 'Good night' through the closed door before going to bed. At least, they had assumed that he was retiring for the night and not leaving the house. They had been too busy giggling and talking about people they knew to have given it much thought. After all, where would he have gone in the middle of the night? All of these thoughts raced through JoJo's head as she sat there wondering what to do next, her hands knotted in her hair. Marcy was looking at her expectantly, breathing short rapid breaths and holding her covers up to her chin as well.

"Go wait out there while we get dressed," JoJo finally decided, waving the little man out of her bedroom with the back of her hand. "Go on!"

He bowed politely, the sad smile never leaving his face as he spun on one heel and noiselessly walked through the doorway. JoJo jumped off her bed, ran to the door and shut it firmly, turning to lean her back against it in case the man tried to get back in. She stared at Marcy in disbelief.

"What the heck are you doing?" she asked.

"Calling my mother," Marcy answered, her phone shaking in one hand while she paused with her finger in mid-air. Her best friend's face told her that that was a mistake. "What?"

"What do you plan to say to her? 'Hi Mom. Yeah, doing great. We woke up this morning and Mr. Mallory's gone God-knows-where and some little man dressed up like the Lucky Charms guy came in our bedroom and scared the bejeebers out of us.' She'd probably call 911 and this place would be swarming with cops and firemen and ambulances."

"Well, that's a lot better than being held hostage by a rogue Leprechaun who wants to do evil things to us…"

Leprechaun? JoJo thought, scrunching her forehead. *Is that what this little fella is?* Taking a deep breath, she said as calmly as she could, "Look, if he wanted to kill us or something, he could've done that while we were asleep. Let's put some clothes on and just go out and listen to him and find out where my Dad went."

"All right," Marcy answered reluctantly, finally pulling the covers off of her, "but I'm keeping my phone ready the whole time, and the instant that something starts looking fishy, I'm calling the police."

They dressed quickly, JoJo pulling on her favorite pair of jeans and a long-sleeve, purplish tee-shirt with a faded picture of a dancing moose on it. As she tugged at her socks and shoved her feet into a pair of worn leather half-boots, she thought about Marcy's phone. Again. Marcy and everyone else her age had their own phone. JoJo's father had decided that she, however, didn't *need* a phone until she was at least a teenager. He obviously had no idea about what kids in the sixth grade needed these days. At any rate, seeing Marcy whip out her phone like it was the most natural thing in the world stung more than a little bit, not that it was her friend's fault.

When they were both ready – Marcy was dressed in her usual baggy sweatshirt and sweatpants that somewhat concealed her extra weight – JoJo carefully opened the door, peeking to see if the Leprechaun was still there. Part of her hoped that he had gone and that this was all just a bad dream or a prank that Dad was playing on them. Just in case it was real, however, she'd grabbed a small baseball bat out of her sister's closet. Marcy was behind her, cell phone at the ready.

"There is little time." The Leprechaun was standing in the middle of the kitchen, about ten feet away from JoJo's bedroom door. Despite knowing he was there, the girls still jumped at the sound of his voice.

"Little time for what? And who *are* you?" JoJo asked, holding the bat in front of her with both hands. The little man raised an eyebrow in amusement at the sight of the weapon, which only caused JoJo's face to redden. Waving the bat from side to side in her best threatening manner, she added, "Don't think for a minute that I won't use this if I need to."

The girls had stopped a good five feet from the Leprechaun, with Marcy staying protectively behind her best friend. Not only was she afraid of whatever the mysterious small man may have in store for them, but she was equally fearful of getting clobbered by JoJo and her bat-waving. JoJo could see the empty unmade bed through the open door of her father's bedroom.

"I am Flick," the Leprechaun began, holding his palms up as if to show his innocence. "They will torture your father until he tells them where it is. If he doesn't know, they will keep going anyway, until he expires. By that time, no one will recognize him, not even you. You must hurry."

"Whoa, slow down a minute!" JoJo stopped waving the bat around. "Who is 'they' and what is 'it' and where is Dad?"

For the first time, Flick seemed uncomfortable, his face drooping heavily. "They are the Gories – the three witch-daughters of Pewtris Grimm – and they seek the *Chrimeus*, Merlin's most powerful magical legacy. They hold your father captive in Shadowrock, the dark fortress."

"Merlin?" Marcy interrupted excitedly, coming around from behind JoJo and placing one hand on the baseball bat to keep it from knocking her in the head. "But that's impossible. He's just a character from the King Arthur stories, along with the Knights of the Round Table and Lady Guinevere and…"

Flick's head snapped up suddenly and he raised a cautionary finger, causing Marcy to stop her impromptu book report. "You must take care with speaking certain names aloud! It is forbidden, and punishable by death if heard by the wrong ears. None more so than the former name of Shadowrock itself."

JoJo shared a knowing look with Marcy, whose lips were pressed tightly together. The threat of *any* kind of punishment – much less death – was enough to keep her mouth shut. JoJo, on the other hand, never could resist a dare. Besides, they were talking about her *father*.

"Camelot? They've taken my Dad to *Camelot*?"

Chapter Two

Strange Partners

Flick cringed at the name spoken aloud by JoJo. Not once, but twice. The Leprechaun half-looked over his shoulder, as if expecting someone to appear out of nowhere to haul Josephine Mallory away to her punishment. Instead, there was a loud knock at the front door, which caused all three of them to jump.

"Wow, they're fast!" Marcy said, terrified at the thought of what was on the other side of the door. She looked at Flick for confirmation. The little man seemed more curious than afraid.

"Marcy, I seriously doubt that they'd be polite enough to knock on the door," JoJo responded, "whoever 'they' are." She rested the baseball bat on her shoulder and headed toward the door.

She had noticed from the kitchen that the back door was still bolted shut from the inside, and now she saw the same with the front door. There was no way that her Dad could have left the house, unless he went out one of the windows. *What's going on?* she thought for the umpteenth time that morning, *and who could be knocking on the door this early on a Saturday?* She peeked through the curtain next to the door and relaxed. Hurriedly, JoJo unfastened the locks and let her visitor in.

"What's with the bat?" An athletic boy with a blond flat-top haircut asked matter-of-factly. He had a pair of skates hanging around his neck and a hockey stick in one hand. "I thought we were gonna skate today."

"You're not going to believe it," JoJo answered, rolling her eyes. "C'mon in."

Marcy's heart sank when she saw who was joining them. She'd almost wished it had been the posse coming to get JoJo for uttering 'Camelot'. Almost. Not *him*, for Pete's sake! Her morning was going from very bad to worse. Why Trip?

Johnny Dowling was JoJo's other best friend in the world. He lived four houses down on the same street, and they'd known each other practically since birth, going to school together every day since pre-k. More importantly, they skated together. Ice hockey skating, not the figure skating that girls like Marcy did. Johnny once scored *nine* goals in a single game – a triple hat trick – earning him the nickname 'Trip'.

At school, Trip was practically worshipped, even by the older kids. Eighth-grade boys wanted to be his friends, and eighth-grade girls wanted to be his girlfriends. 'Normal' sixth-graders got treated like dirt by the upper grades at Mahoney Middle School, but not Trip. The funny thing was that he didn't seem to care about the attention at all. To JoJo, he was just the guy she grew up skinning her knees with. To Marcy, Trip was a cocky, arrogant Jock. To Trip, Marcy simply didn't exist.

Following JoJo into the kitchen, he pulled up short when he noticed Flick for the first time. "What's with the midget?"

"He's a Leprechaun, not a midget," Marcy corrected in a loud whisper, as if Flick couldn't hear her. "Oh, and by the way, hello to you, too."

Trip looked from Flick to Marcy's expectant face and then back, his lips pressed tightly together like he was in serious thought. "A Leprechaun? Cool. Aren't they supposed to have pots of gold or something?"

Marcy blew out a breath in exasperation. Her face was amazingly red already.

"This one woke us up to tell us that my Dad's been kidnapped by witches and taken away to Camelot, only it's not Camelot anymore," JoJo explained matter-of-factly. Flick and Marcy both cringed each time she said the name, but she shrugged them off.

"Where's everyone else?" Trip asked, looking around the small house in one sweeping turn of his head. "Did they take your sisters, too?"

"I wish. No, they're all at friends' houses. They don't even know yet. Heck, I'm not even sure what *I* know yet." JoJo rubbed her head with one hand, the other still hanging on to the bat.

Marcy cleared her throat loudly. "I think it's time I called my Mom. She'll know what to do." She waved her phone to indicate her intention.

"Your mom do a lot of work with Leprechauns and witches and stuff?" Trip asked, looking curiously at Marcy as if he'd just noticed her for the first time.

"My mother is an *engineer*…"

"There is little time." Again the warning from Flick.

Trip hadn't heard Flick speak up to this point, and the deepness of the Leprechaun's voice caught him by surprise.

"Already, they torture him for news of the *Chrimeus*," Flick continued solemnly. "Soon, he will crumble."

"What do you mean, 'crumble'?" JoJo demanded, almost shouting. "If he doesn't know what they want or where it is, then how can they expect him to *tell* them?"

Flick looked at her sadly. "If he does not know what they seek – like all those before him – they would torture him anyway, until his life seeps painfully away." He hesitated to make sure he had their complete attention. "But they will take as much time with your father as need be, making sure to keep him miserably alive just long enough."

"Long enough for what?" Trip asked before either of the others had a chance.

"To tell them what they wish to know."

"How's he supposed to do that?" JoJo asked, her heart already racing. "How in the world is my Dad supposed to know anything about this stupid magic thingamajig when we live here and all that stuff happened in Camelot, or whatever you call it now?" She looked at Marcy to confirm that she was on the right track.

"And, technically speaking, Cam- uh… Shadowrock is just a fictional place," Marcy added, picking up the cue from JoJo. "So nothing *real* happened there at all. King Arthur and the Knights of the Round Table, Merlin, Guinevere – all that was just a story made up for our entertainment. There's no such thing as magic."

Flick folded his arms across his chest and stared grimly at the two girls and Trip. He appeared to be considering what JoJo and Marcy said. Very slowly and deliberately he unfolded his arms and held his hands out in front of him, palms facing inward toward each other. Without saying a word, a ball of swirling mist began to form in the space between his hands, growing from the size of a golf ball until it was as big as the Leprechaun's head. The three kids watched, mesmerized, holding their breaths.

The mist began to clear away, revealing a large glass ball suspended in the middle of the air, Flick's hands just an inch or so away on either side. The glass was unlike anything JoJo and her friends had ever seen, multicolored at one instant, then crystal clear the next. It had a sparkling quality to it that reminded them of the sun shining through a tall glass of fizzy water. Within the ball, objects began to form, somewhat blurry at first, then becoming much clearer. A cell phone. A baseball bat. A hockey stick and pair of skates.

"What the…?" Trip hadn't even noticed that he was no longer holding his stick or that his skates weren't draped around his neck any more.

"Hey, give me back my phone!" Marcy demanded.

JoJo examined her empty hands in disbelief, never having felt the bat leave her grasp. When she looked back at the glass ball, she noticed it was shrinking.

"Can we have our stuff back now?" Trip asked when the sphere reached the point where it was the size of a baseball. Before he could say another word, the glass ball suddenly condensed to a bright dot, like when turning off a television, and disappeared altogether. "Whoa, that can't be good!"

"My phone!" Marcy screamed.

JoJo was not as concerned about her little sister's baseball bat as her friends were about their items, and for good reason. Like all sixth-graders *not* named Josephine Mallory, Marcy loved her phone and spent hours on it every day. Texting, Snapchat, Tumblr, the usual stuff. As important as that was to Marcy, the hockey gear was a hundred times more significant to Trip, part of the very definition of who he was. He also had a phone – of course – but could go days without using it. On the other hand, he felt naked without his skates and stick.

"Okay, you made your point," JoJo finally said. "There's such a thing as magic. Obviously, you got in here somehow without breaking a window, and the trick with the glass ball was pretty neat. Can you please return our stuff now before my friends go absolutely ballistic?"

Flick bowed wordlessly. When he rose, he waved one small hand and the missing objects reappeared in their original places – in hands or around necks. It was hard to tell who was more relieved between Marcy and Trip because he didn't wear his emotions like she did, to say the least.

"The magic of a Leprechaun is nothing compared to the sorcery commanded by the Gories who have your father. And the dark wizardry of Pewtris Grimm vastly outweighs the combined magic of his witch-daughters. The *Chrimeus*, however, is more powerful than even Grimm, which is why he is so committed to finding it. Your father has that information, and it is only a matter of time before he reveals it to the witches. Your only hope is to bring the *Chrimeus* to Shadowrock, and trade it for your father before it is too late."

JoJo stared at Flick, waiting for more. When he didn't continue, she looked at her friends to see if she had missed something. Their blank faces said they knew as little as she did.

"I don't get it," she said to Flick. "How in the heck are we supposed to find this *Chrimeus* thing, and then get it to a place that's not even in our world, all in time to save my Dad from getting tortured?"

Flick tilted his head to one side, as if she'd said something peculiar. "First of all, you must go to Erristan in order to locate the *Chrimeus*. Before you depart, it would be wise to see if your father left any clues or guidance, regarding the *Chrimeus'* location. Last, and most sadly, I'm afraid we cannot *completely* save your father from torture. That process has undoubtedly already begun."

The last sentence hit JoJo like a punch in the stomach. She tried to breathe, but the thought of her poor father…

"One thing still doesn't make sense," Marcy said, feeling more confident now that she had her phone back. "Why would *JoJo's Dad* know anything about this *Chrimeus* thing in the first place?"

Flick folded his hands together in front of him, almost like he was praying. Looking straight at JoJo, as if she were the one who had asked the question, he replied, "Because he is the one who hid the *Chrimeus* when he lived in our world."

Chapter Three

Clues

"What are we looking for again?" Trip asked for at least the third time as he moved knick-knacks around on shelves in the Mallorys' small living room.

"Anything that might say where this stupid *Chrimeus* is hidden," JoJo yelled from her father's bedroom. She was very uncomfortable going through his things, never before having spent any time alone in this room. The only time she remembered ever coming in here before was with her sisters when they made breakfast for Dad on his birthday. She wished she could find whatever she was looking for and be out of here. Then again, what she really wished was that she didn't have to be doing this in the first place.

JoJo had decided against calling her older sisters, Maggie and Ronnie, because she really didn't want to go through the hassle of trying to explain everything, especially when she wasn't all that sure herself. Not to mention, they just plain wouldn't believe her. Leprechauns, magic, Camelot... seriously? Oh yeah, and by the way, Dad supposedly had a life in a different world. She would just leave them a note instead, saying something about going away with her friends for a few days. Just this once it was convenient *not* having a cell phone because they wouldn't be able to track her down.

Convincing Marcy to *not* call her mother had taken a lot of persuasion. Marcy was both positive that her engineer-Mom would have all the answers, and afraid not to tell her what was going on. In the end, JoJo had simply threatened to leave Marcy behind if she spilled the beans to anyone, including and especially Mrs. DiPietro. They would concoct some story about going camping and ice-fishing with JoJo's Dad for the next few days, and hope that Marcy's mother bought off on it. But Marcy would have to wait until the very last minute to text her and let her know.

Trip was another matter altogether. If he said he was hanging out with JoJo for the next three or four days, his mother wouldn't bat an eyelash. She worked two jobs and often went that long without seeing her son, but she didn't feel a need to worry about him. Every policeman in town knew who the young hockey star was, and they'd all ensure that nothing would endanger his very promising future. The boy had never been a trouble-maker like some of his buddies because creating mischief took too much time and energy away from perfecting his game.

"Hey, I think I might have found something!" Marcy hollered from the kitchen. JoJo gladly stopped rummaging through her Dad's nightstand and hurried to go see what her friend had discovered. Trip sauntered over from the living room, curious as well, but not seeing a need to run.

Marcy was holding up the oddest-looking key that any of them had ever seen. It appeared to actually be two keys welded together, side by side at their heads in such a way that it would take a long, narrow opening for the key to fit into.

"Where'd you find this?" JoJo asked, accepting the key and looking it over more closely. On one side, there were no inscriptions of any kind, not even the maker of whatever lock this went to. On the other was scratched the words "stone wall" in very small letters.

"In this drawer," Marcy answered, pointing with the back of her hand. "I thought that it must be something special because it was actually taped to the bottom of the silverware holder."

"What does it go to?" Trip asked. If he was impressed that she found the odd key, he wasn't showing it.

JoJo turned the key over and over, trying to imagine if she'd ever seen a lock or keyhole that would accept the bizarre piece of metal. "I don't have a clue," she said finally, looking at both of her friends.

"Yes, you do," Marcy responded. "Let's go down to your father's office."

JoJo shot her a quizzical look. Not many people even knew about the room in the basement, much less would have a reason for wanting to go down there. She shrugged and headed to the door that led to the cellar office, her friends trailing after her. As she pulled the door open, she half-hoped that the light would be on and that her Dad was downstairs reading after all. Her heart sank when all she saw was darkness.

"Hey, where'd that little dude go?" Trip asked, looking around before following the girls down the narrow wooden staircase.

It was a good question. In their frantic search for clues no one had noticed that Flick had disappeared. They had all assumed that he was going to lead them to this Erristan place, and on to Shadowrock as kind of a guide. Without the Leprechaun, they had absolutely no idea of how to get where they were supposed to go.

The three of them spilled into the long single basement room that served as both an office and a small library of sorts. Bookcases lined the walls, some going all the way to the low ceiling, while others stopped about halfway up. Mr. Mallory loved to read, especially books about history. History of people. History of places. History of can-openers. It didn't matter. It was almost as if he was determined to learn the entire history of mankind as quickly and thoroughly as he could. If he was watching television, you could bet it would be on the History channel. If what Flick had said about him coming here from another world was true, then the obsession with *this world's* history made a little sense.

On the walls above the shorter bookcases were large, cheaply framed pictures of various historical events – Washington crossing the Delaware, Ben Franklin flying a kite, the Wright Brothers at Kitty Hawk, and others. At the far end of the room, in front of a worn-out leather reading chair, was a painting of a Confederate officer on a gray horse. The man had a fiercely determined look on his face and was holding his sword out defiantly. Marcy walked straight over and read the name just above the bottom of the frame: BG Thomas Jonathan Jackson, CSA. Smiling, she turned to face the others, holding her hand up to the picture, "May I present, Stonewall Jackson."

"Nice job, Marcy," JoJo said, genuinely impressed. "I wouldn't have gotten that in a million years."

"Longer for me," Trip added. He knew his strengths, and neither history nor puzzle-solving fell into that category. While he didn't actually congratulate Marcy for putting the pieces together, it was the closest thing to a compliment from him that she figured on getting. "So, how does the key work on it?"

In answer to his question, they all began searching the painting and frame for telltale openings that might allow for the bizarre key. Trip even tried pulling the entire frame away from the wall, but it wouldn't budge.

"Wait a minute, guys," JoJo said suddenly, squatting down slightly and squinting back up at the picture. "I think I see something. In the shadow of the thing that holds the sword – "

"Scabbard," Marcy supplied, "and it's technically a saber, not a sword."

"And that's important because?" Trip half-mumbled without looking at her. JoJo was used to being corrected by her older sisters, her father, and her best friend. Clearly, Trip was not.

"Whatever," JoJo said to quickly defuse the situation, and lined the key up with a long, skinny hole in the painting that was hidden about halfway up the scabbard, but barely visible, even once they found it. "Let's see what we get here…"

Click! They all jumped back, startled by the sound, even though it wasn't all that loud. JoJo hadn't had to turn the key one way or the other, the correct insertion into the keyhole and the right amount of pressure being enough to do the trick. The picture – frame and all – swung slowly away from the wall, revealing a small rectangular opening. It was a little too high up for JoJo and Marcy to be able to see, even on their tip-toes, but Trip was a couple of inches taller than either of the girls.

"There's a rolled-up piece of paper and a little box in there," he said, peering into the dark space. "Want me to get 'em?"

He didn't wait for an answer, reaching in and removing first the roll, which was soft and made of something other than paper. More like a cured animal skin of some sort. It was sealed with a very thin disc of red wax with an impression in the middle of it. Trip handed the roll to JoJo and retrieved the small wooden box next. It was seamless, with no obvious way to open it. For the time being, he just held it, waiting to hear what was next.

"Let's take a look at the scroll first," Marcy suggested, excited that it might contain ancient academic writings. "You might want to be careful with that wax…"

JoJo broke the seal open without hesitation, bits of wax falling to the floor. She looked at Marcy and shrugged her shoulders as if to say, *"Oops!"*, and then proceeded to unroll the parchment. It turned out to be a square, about a foot long on each side.

"A map?" JoJo asked, turning it first one way, and then the other. She held it in a way that the others could see it better, especially Marcy. "Does this make any sense to you?"

Trip didn't feel offended. He wasn't naïve enough to expect anyone to ask him questions like this, especially when they had a brainiac in the group. He had a pretty good idea of where most of the major hockey cities were, but that was about all the geography he knew.

Marcy took a few extra seconds, but it seemed a lot longer. Finally, her eyes opened wide as if she'd just realized the answer to a tough test question. "I think this is a map of the inside of Shadowrock. I don't know what this writing at the bottom is all about. Some kind of code, maybe."

"Shadowrock?" Trip asked, confused. "What's that?"

"It's Camelot," JoJo provided, "but they'll take away your birthday if they hear you calling it that, so we have to say Shadowrock now. What's in the box?"

He gave the box a twist, and nothing happened. Holding it up and turning it over and around, Trip could find no indication of how it was supposed to open. The grain of the wood had no visible changes or interruptions that might point to a way to gain access to the inside of the container. He squeezed the sides to see if it would simply pop open, but again without success. Finally, out of options, he pushed the end of his pinky finger straight in against one end, and he felt it give. He continued to apply pressure as a very small drawer slid out the opposite end. He tipped the contents into his other hand and held it out for the others to see.

Another weird key.

Chapter Four

A Small Guide

"What is it with the goofy keys?" JoJo said to no one in particular.

Trip was still holding the latest version, which featured a cubic shape at the end that figured to go into whatever lock it was designed for. It was made of a coarse-looking metal with a diamond-shaped handle, like it could have gone to the massive front door of a giant cathedral.

"Any writing on this one?" Marcy asked. "I mean, is there anything to point what it might go to?" She strained to get a good look at it, and Trip finally got the unspoken message to surrender it to her. Marcy anxiously spun the key in her hand, searching for any clue that might lead to where they needed to go next. Nothing.

Now that JoJo had the map and Marcy was holding the key, Trip found his hands once again empty. He reached back into the small opening in the wall to make sure they weren't leaving anything behind, stretching his fingers as far back as they would go. He felt something soft, like a piece of fabric of some sort.

"Hey, there's more," he announced to the girls, who immediately turned their attention to what he was doing. "It feels like a piece of cloth… hold on… got it!"

When he retracted his hand from the hole, he was pinching between two of fingers a small purple mesh pouch, maybe twice the size of a tea-bag. The pouch had been drawn closed, and tiny yellow ribbons hung down from what could only be the top. With surprising dexterity, Trip undid the drawstrings and gently pulled the pouch open.

A gold-and-black butterfly fluttered out, suddenly free after who knows how long. The beautiful creature was only slightly bigger than a quarter, although it was hard to tell exactly because it flew around like butterflies do. Trip attempted to catch it in his cupped hands, but JoJo grabbed his arm.

"Don't. I've got to believe that that butterfly was locked away in there for a reason. If you smash him in your hands accidentally, we won't know what that reason is."

Instead, they followed the colorful insect to the other end of the room. Like the rest of the office, this end held bookcases filled with books of all sizes. For the most part, the books were fairly neatly placed on the shelves. Perhaps Mr. Mallory had a system for organizing them in a way that made sense to him. Not as complicated as regular libraries, but still a way to keep track of what went where. The kids, even JoJo, didn't know if there was such a system here, and it was doubtful that any of them would care. So that when the butterfly finally landed, they thought that it had been completely random. JoJo squatted to get a better look.

She laughed and pulled the book out, standing back up with it so that the others could see.

Merlin Through the Years. No author.

"Are we supposed to read it?" Marcy and Trip asked at the same time, although certainly not with the same degree of enthusiasm. Marcy looked like she couldn't wait to devour whatever was written inside. That's the way she was with any book. Trip, on the other hand, treated it like it was a poisonous snake.

"I don't know," JoJo answered. Looking down at the spot on the shelf where the book had been, she said, "I wonder why the butterfly keeps flying in and out of there."

Trip went down on one knee so that he could look into the dark space between books. He took his phone out, and quickly turned the built-in flashlight on to help him see better. He squinted as he moved the light around. After a second or two, he looked back up excitedly at the two girls. He stuck his empty hand out to Marcy.

"Hey… uh…"

"'Marcy'. It's 'Marcy'. For crying out loud, you don't even know my *name*, do you?"

"Well, I kind of just met you, you know," Trip replied, not the least bit embarrassed.

"We've been going to the same school together since last fall!" she screamed at him. "I sit right *next* to you in fourth-period History with Mrs. Unger, and right in *front* of you in sixth-period English with Mr. Towle."

Trip grinned. "Then you can't expect me to recognize you if I've been staring at the back of your head all year, right?" Thinking that this conversation was finished, he asked, "Now, can I have that key, please?"

Red-faced, Marcy thrust the odd-shaped key at him in a way that might have been dangerous if it had been a foot or so longer. JoJo watched in stifled amusement as Trip took the key without another word. She knew that he didn't like to argue, or even be around people who raised their voices. She was also very aware of Marcy's strong desire to fit in with all of the right groups, and how being invisible made it twice as hard.

Trip pulled a couple of books from either side of gap created by the missing Merlin book, and set them on the floor, giving him enough room to stick his hand into the space. Lining the key up with the help of the flashlight, he extended it forward into what looked like a diamond-shaped dark space. Once it felt securely inserted, he gave it a turn and felt the lock respond. "Score!"

Before Trip could stand up, the entire bookcase began rotating into the wall, pivoting on its right-hand edge like a book-filled door. Once it stopped, they were staring at a gloomy narrow passageway with dust-covered stairs leading downward. They couldn't see more than three or four steps before the darkness completely swallowed the light from the office.

"Whoa! Where do you think this goes?" Trip asked, shining his flashlight into the shadows. It penetrated a few feet further than the room light. The girls moved up beside him to peek inside. There didn't seem to be any walls on either side, or a ceiling that they could see. Just steps that kept going down.

Before anyone could answer, the butterfly flew past the three of them into the blackness and out of sight, quickly out of range of Trip's flashlight.

"I'm guessing that this takes us to where we can find my Dad," JoJo replied, more bravely than she felt. "And once we get there we'll have to figure out how to use that map and whatever gibberish is at the bottom of it."

"We're not going to just go in there, are we?" Marcy asked in a squeaky, trembling voice. "I can't go in there without calling my mother. She's not going to be real happy if I just take off and she can't get a hold of me, and I'm assuming that we won't be getting real good phone service wherever we're headed."

JoJo and Trip shared a look. They'd been through all of this already and didn't want to have to listen again to what Marcy's mother would have to say about their plans. Leading the way with his flashlight-phone, Trip climbed down onto the first step.

"Look Marcy, if you don't want to go, you don't have to, but don't you *dare* tell anyone where we went, including your mom. And if you're not coming with us, I'm going to need that map," JoJo said solemnly, her open hand reaching out. Trip had descended another couple of steps.

Marcy stared at her best friend's expectant hand, knowing full well that if she surrendered the map it meant she'd decided to stay behind. She also knew that neither JoJo nor Trip would have much chance of deciphering whatever riddles were written on the parchment, no matter how hard they tried. Worst, she realized that when all the kids at school eventually found out about this stupendous adventure, one of the story lines would be about how Marcy DiPietro bailed out because she was worried that her mother disapproved. She would go from being completely unknown to being famous as the *lamest* kid in the entire school! Staring at the phone in her other hand, she reached over and pushed one of its buttons. JoJo cringed.

"You know, it would've been nice to eat before we take off," she said, smiling at JoJo as the flashlight from her phone shone brightly. "Go ahead – I'm right behind you. As if I was going to let you and Mister Hockey Stick have all the fun!"

JoJo breathed a sigh of relief and followed Trip into the shadowy passageway, carefully picking her way down the steps. Of course, she would have gone without Marcy because her father needed her, but she was glad that the smartest person in all of sixth grade was going with them. The bouncing light behind her announced that Marcy was indeed following her closely.

JoJo reached out to the sides from time to time as they continued to make their way down the staircase, but her hands never found anything solid to touch. The light from the two phones didn't penetrate much more than a few feet, barely showing them where the next step was, but revealing nothing else about the strange passageway. The air was musty and old-smelling, like an abandoned warehouse that had been sealed up against the outside for years and years.

"We've got a problem," Trip announced, coming to an abrupt stop. "Looks like the end of the road."

"What do you mean?" The panic in Marcy's voice was clear as she barely avoided a collision with JoJo.

"No more stairs." He waved his light around, searching for something solid to step on. "It's just all black... air, I guess. What's that noise?"

A sound like salt or flour pouring out of a bag softly began filtering through the space. Marcy and Trip moved their flashlights around wildly, searching for the source of the noise. Her piercing screech told the others that Marcy had found it.

"What is it?" JoJo asked, whipping her head back and forth to see what had caused the unnerving scream.

"The stairs we just came down are… are *dissolving!* It's like they're just turning into sand!"

Without another word, the steps under their feet fell away into dust and disappeared, and JoJo, Trip, and Marcy fell into the blackness.

Chapter Five

Bearings

Their screams were gobbled up by the darkness as they tumbled blindly through the ink-black. JoJo had managed to grab each of her friends by their shirts just as their footing had vanished, and now held on for dear life.

Trip was the first to stop making noise, followed closely by JoJo. Marcy continued to alternate between squeals and prayers and apologies to her mother for having gone off on this ridiculous adventure without her permission.

Still, they continued to fall through a void that didn't seem to be ending anytime soon. JoJo was convinced that they'd all be killed by the landing, given how fast they must be dropping. *There's no way in the world we're gonna survive this*, she thought as she re-tightened her grip on her friends. Her hands and forearms began to ache.

Boomph!

They landed hard, knocking the wind out of all three of them, but somehow nothing worse than that. No broken legs or cracked skulls. JoJo opened her eyes, not realizing that she had closed them, and was surprised to see the sun shining overhead. Underneath her, the ground where they had plopped down was soft and spongy, covered with clover and small yellow flowers. *Thank goodness for that*, was the first thought that ran through her head and she let go of the others' shirts and sat up.

"Hey, you guys okay?" she said, looking first to Marcy and then at Trip, who was lying on his back, actually smiling. "What's so funny?"

"That we're still alive," he answered, the grin fixed on his face as he stared up at the sky. "You know, it wasn't even that hard of a landing. I've been popped a lot worse than that on the ice."

"Yeah, me too," JoJo agreed, happy to see he was all right. Turning back to Marcy, who was definitely *not* smiling, she asked again, "You okay, Marcy?"

"I don't see anything *funny* about any of this," she spat out, climbing to her hands and knees. "And, of course, I landed on my phone." She showed the shattered front of her cell phone to the others.

"Ha! At least you still have yours," Trip said, finally getting to his feet. "I dropped mine somewhere while we were falling through outer space or wherever we were."

Marcy looked at Trip and hated him all over again. How could anyone who just went through what they experienced be smiling? He's acting like this is something normal in his life, for crying out loud! She stood up and tried to power her phone on, managing to cut her finger on the broken glass instead. Disgusted, she threw the device on the ground and stepped on it angrily.

"I figured you for the no-trash, save-the-planet type," Trip said watching her. Without giving her a chance to respond, he turned away and looked around at their new environment. "Where do you think we are?"

JoJo winced and shook her head as she watched Marcy's neck and face turn scarlet. On the one hand, she was somewhat glad that no one had a phone now, and she didn't have to feel like a misfit about it. On the other, however, she needed to make sure her best friend didn't blow a gasket. She put her arm around Marcy and gave her a squeeze.

"Calm down, Marcy," she said gently. "Everything's going to be fine, trust me."

Marcy pulled away suddenly, her eyes large as she looked at JoJo. "Trust you? That's how I got into this mess in the first place, and now I don't even have a phone!"

"Welcome to my world," JoJo answered, punching the other girl playfully on the arm. It wasn't something Marcy was used to, and she made a face while rubbing at the imagined pain.

Trip had begun to wander away, now about twenty feet from where the girls stood. They were in the middle of a big field that was spread over a large rounded mound. There were trees in several directions, and beyond them the land rolled with gentle hills and valleys, all displaying vibrant spring colors. Off in the distance, they could barely make out dark gray mountains lined up like guards.

"Well, it's definitely not Maine," Trip pronounced unnecessarily, turning back to face the girls. When they had gotten up that morning, it was still the middle of winter in their hometown, with no leaves on the trees and no flowers on the ground.

Marcy had a smart-aleck remark all ready, but – with a great deal of self-control – bit it off before it left her mouth. No matter how much she disliked the Jock, making fun of his ignorance wasn't going to go over well with JoJo. Besides, she realized that she didn't actually know where they were, either.

"What do you want to do?" JoJo asked both of her friends, turning from one to the other so that no one felt left out. "I mean, we can't just start wandering around without some kind of plan, right?"

"I think we should ask the smart girl." Trip offered. When Marcy eyed him suspiciously, he added, "Marcy."

"I guess that must make me 'the dumb girl'," JoJo muttered, loud enough for the others to hear. Trip wasn't worried that he'd actually hurt her feelings because they'd called each other names ever since they could talk. He didn't think this was any different.

Marcy ignored JoJo's comment while she thought about their situation. Academically, she knew she was as strong as Trip was at hockey. Well, almost. This predicament didn't call for a scholarly answer, however. It was more common sense and coming up with a strategy.

"Okay, the first thing we need to find out is where we are, and to do that we need to find a person or a sign. So, if we can locate a house or road, we should be able to able to answer that question. Assuming, of course, that they speak English here. Next, we have to determine how far it is to Shadowrock, again assuming we're even in the right country… or kingdom. Third, we will have to find the fastest way to get us from here to the castle." She paused to see if the others agreed with her plan.

"See, I told you we should listen to the smart girl," Trip said, grinning again at JoJo. "Of course, you're a smart girl, too…"

"Yeah, yeah. Save it, Bozo." JoJo headed toward a single tree growing near the middle of the mound. "At least I know who the best tree-climber in this group is."

The others followed, stopping at the base of the tree and looking up to see what JoJo would be faced with. The trunk was massive, at least eight feet across, and huge limbs grew out of its sides not too far from the ground. It was a giant oak that had been around for well over a century, but the kids could care less about any of that. JoJo wasted no time, quickly and easily scrambling up onto one of the huge lower branches. She surveyed the part of the tree closest to her, determining what her next move would be, never looking back down at her friends.

"You know what you're doing?" Trip asked teasingly. He knew he was lucky that she didn't have anything to throw at him.

"Be careful," Marcy said, meaning it. It's what her mother would have said, had she been there. Actually, her mom would have probably said to stay out of the tree altogether. In some ways, JoJo was lucky not to have a mother watching over her constantly.

Marcy felt guilty almost immediately for having thought like that. She knew, better than just about anybody, how much the absence of her mother tore at her best friend. JoJo had been five years old when it was said that her Mom jumped off the big Million Dollar Bridge going into Portland. Some people said she was pushed, but no one was ever arrested. Worse yet, the body was never found. As far Marcy knew, Mrs. Mallory had not left behind a note, which is what people committing suicide always seem to do. JoJo hardly ever talked about her any more, but she did get on Marcy whenever her friend started complaining too much about her own mother.

"Can you see anything yet?" Trip hollered up to her. JoJo was already more than halfway up the humongous tree, a good fifty feet off the ground.

"Not yet," she shouted back down. "Gimme a minute until I can get higher."

Marcy envied the ease and enthusiasm that JoJo displayed while climbing, as if it was the most natural thing in the world for her. She knew she'd be paralyzed with fear to be that high up. *Heck*, she thought, *I'd never make it off the first branch!*

JoJo negotiated her way near the very top of the oak. She searched for the spot that would give her the best view of the surrounding countryside, which was the whole reason for this exercise. Moving her feet carefully, she tested a thin branch to see if it was sturdy enough before continuing. The last thing she wanted was to hear the crack of tree limb at this point, followed by her unplanned rapid descent. The branch held, and she shifted her weight accordingly. Reaching with one hand, JoJo pulled aside a small leafy branch that was blocking her view.

"Got it," she said, mostly to herself. JoJo was afraid that any effort to yell down to the others would knock her off-balance, so they'd just have to wait a few minutes to hear her report. She shifted her attention back to which branch to grab and where to step as she started her way back down to her waiting friends.

"Well?" Trip asked anxiously before she was halfway to the ground. "What'd you see?"

"Give her a chance to get down first, will you?" Marcy scolded.

"Quit acting like such a grandma," Trip shot back, shaking his head without actually looking at her. If he had, he would have seen the redness reappearing all across her face.

JoJo hopped lightly to the ground and brushed her hands together. She was beaming from the exhilaration of the climb, but was happy to be back down. From Marcy's pouty face and Trip's impish grin, she could tell that something had been said while she was gone. Probably a lot of somethings.

"There's a bunch of houses – like a village or something – right over that way," she announced, pointing. "It didn't look too far, so we oughtta be able to get there pretty fast."

"Great," Trip chirped, starting to jog in the direction she indicated. "Let's get going!"

"Great," Marcy moaned as she watched JoJo run off after him. Grudgingly, she made herself do the one thing she absolutely hated.

Chapter Six

Renegades

JoJo and Trip slowed to a stop – again – and waited for Marcy to catch up. Even though they had given up on running because she had no prayer of keeping up with them, they now found that she was falling behind when they simply walked. Neither Trip nor JoJo showed any signs of exertion, much less fatigue. Marcy, on the other hand, looked to be just about ready to collapse.

"How much further?" she moaned as she finally caught up to them, practically dragging her feet in the process. Her face was flushed and little streams of sweat ran down its sides, disappearing into her baggy sweatshirt.

JoJo looked back in the direction that they'd started from, and then toward where she figured the houses to be. They'd only been moving for a little over an hour, as best as she could guess. In her hurry to get dressed that morning, she'd forgotten to strap on her wrist watch. Of course, none of her friends needed such a thing because they all carried cell phones. Usually.

"If I'm guessing right, we should be getting close," she replied hopefully. Trip shot her a questioning look, and she answered it silently with one that told him to keep his mouth shut. If she answered Marcy truthfully – that, at this rate, they were probably no more than halfway – she was afraid that her slow-footed friend would just give up and plop down on the ground.

"Oh, good!" Marcy cheered up a little. "Because I don't know how much more of this I can do."

Trip rolled his eyes unsympathetically, and starting walking again in the same direction they'd been heading in since entering the trees. JoJo had lined them up as best she could when they came down off the mound, before starting through the woods. Now, it was just a matter of keeping their bearing without the aid of a compass. Going around trees and rocks, and over ditches, and through bushes bumped them off of their intended course without their knowing it. Amazingly, they made as many deviations in one direction as the other, the end result being that they actually maintained their desired line pretty accurately.

"Hey, I think I see something!" Trip half-shouted back to the girls. He didn't want to make any more noise than was necessary, in case it turned out that they weren't welcome. Patiently waiting for the others to catch up, he stopped and studied what he'd discovered.

JoJo had taken to walking just in front of Marcy, in an effort to keep her friend from falling too far behind or feeling like she was left out. The effect was mostly positive, as Marcy maintained a steady – although very slow – pace. As they pulled up to Trip, JoJo was anxious to see what he'd spotted.

"See on the other side of the field?" he said, pointing through the few trees between them and a wide expanse of farmland. The kids appeared to be on the edge of someone's planted field, whatever crops they were growing just now starting to sprout up out of the ground. Wisps of smoke curled into the air above what looked like a tall wooden fence across the field.

"Let's go see what they can tell us," JoJo said, stepping out of the trees and onto a narrow path between planted rows.

"I hope we can get something to eat," Marcy complained, scrambling to keep up with JoJo's excited pace. "You know, we never even had breakfast this morning. I'm starving."

Trip tried to ignore her, but couldn't resist teasing. "Really? I had a bowl of cereal and a couple of Pop-Tarts before I left the house. I'd have brought you guys some if I'd known…"

"Shut up, Trip!" Marcy barked at him. Saying it made her feel good, although she wasn't used to going around telling people to do that. Her parents would certainly not approve. Still, the words gave her a sense of power, that maybe she was every bit the super-Jock's equal.

As they crossed the field, they got a clearer view of the fence, which turned out to be more like a wall. It was indeed tall, rising about twenty feet and made of rough timbers. There was one small doorway that they could see, and it was open. They didn't see any people yet, but they figured that would change once they were inside. It actually happened before that.

"Halt! Stop right there!" The man's voice came from the top of the wall. JoJo and her friends did as he commanded, stopping a good fifty feet from the open doorway. They had just stepped off of the footpath that threaded the field, and were standing on a stretch of grass that extended all the way to the base of the wall.

"At least they speak English," Marcy muttered under her breath. Of the three, she was the only one who had really considered the possibility that language might be a problem. The others just assumed that everyone speaks English, no matter what country or planet they were on. Marcy was well aware, of course, that the legend of Camelot and King Arthur had all been set in England, but that didn't mean that that's where they were now. They would find out in a minute or two.

"Hello there!" JoJo waved up to the man, who looked to be wearing a hat of some sort. He was also holding what appeared to be a long spear. "We're a little lost, and were hoping that someone could help point us the right way."

"Don't forget to ask if there's a place to grab a bite to eat," Marcy added, her head down so that the man couldn't see that she was talking. JoJo *Shhh'd!* her in response.

The man turned away from them and began shouting something toward the inside of the walled-in place. JoJo strained to hear what he was saying, but neither she nor the others could make it out. When the lookout faced them again, he was joined by two other men up on the wall. One of these was holding a bow with an arrow already fitted and partly pulled back.

Trip and Marcy reflexively put up their hands and went into a crouch, turning their heads away as a protective instinct. JoJo, for some reason, didn't feel as immediately threatened. Maybe if the archer had the arrow drawn all the way and was pointing it directly at them...

"Stay there until your escort arrives!" the third man ordered, apparently the one in charge. He was not carrying a spear or a bow-and-arrow that JoJo could see.

"Escort?" Trip said, not loud enough for any but the girls to hear. "What do you think that's all about?"

Neither of the girls answered. They were too busy keeping an eye on the man with the loaded bow while also watching to see who came out of the doorway to meet them. It didn't take long.

Two tall, rough-looking men appeared through the opening in the wall. They were dressed in raggedy clothes that looked to be constructed from pieces of old burlap sacks, with pants that were held up by lengths of rope tied off like crude belts. Their hair was pulled back and braided into long ponytails, secured with strips of leather. Something strange was plastered to the side of their necks, right below the ear, but it was difficult to tell from this distance. The men didn't appear to be overly muscular, but that didn't mean that Trip and the girls wanted to mess with them. Especially considering the rusty swords each one was carrying.

The two men walked straight toward JoJo and her friends, but showed a hesitant kind of caution that didn't make much sense to the sixth-graders. It was almost as if the armed men were somewhat afraid of a few twelve-year olds.

"What are you children doing out here?" One of the men asked gruffly, as the pair stopped about ten feet short, pointing their swords threateningly. He was the older of the two by quite a bit, going by the scraggly gray whiskers covering his face. The other looked to be not much more than a boy, maybe eighteen at the oldest. Instead of facial hair, pimples dotted his chin and cheeks. The sword in his hand was actually shaking as he stared wide-eyed. The oddity on the sides of their necks turned out to be large, black hoop earrings, dangling from their right ears only.

"We're looking for something to eat," Marcy blurted out before anyone else had a chance to say anything. "Nothing fancy. You know, pastries or pancakes or a nice frittata? Pizza's okay, too, but we just –"

"That's *not* what we're doing," JoJo interrupted, making a slashing motion with her hand that made the younger man jump back. "We were hoping that someone could help us with directions, and then we'll just be on our way. The last thing we want to do is cause any trouble."

"Yeah," Trip added, "and could you please ask the guy with the bow-and-arrow up there to relax a little?"

The pimply-faced guard peered intently at the three strangely dressed children, but their brightly-colored and well-made clothing was not the main focus of his attention. Circling around them, but keeping a safe distance, his stares were aimed solely at their heads, as if there was something odd about...

"Where are your LifeStones?" he asked in a quavering voice as he returned to his starting point. Turning to his senior partner, he announced, "Albie, they've got *no LifeStones!*"

The older man – Albie – stiffened. Pointing his sword at the girls, he commanded, "Lift up your hair and show us your ears. Both of you – do it now!"

Somewhat confused, but definitely not wanting to see these crazy men get any angrier than they already were, JoJo and Marcy looked at one another, shrugged, and pulled their hair up with both hands, exposing their ears. Marcy had tiny gold studs in her lobes, barely visible to the guards, while JoJo had nothing. Like the cell phone, she was deemed 'not old enough' to get her ears pierced yet.

"See? It's like I said!" the younger guard said excitedly. "All three of 'em."

JoJo, Marcy, and Trip exchanged looks that said *What the heck is going on?* Before they could get a clear answer, Albie gave them another order.

"Put your hands up in the air, all of you. Now!" Turning to the young guard, he added, "Get around behind them, Barney, and make sure they don't try to make a run for it."

The teenager did as he was told, keeping a wide berth between him and the odd, young visitors until he was between them and the field they had just crossed. He nervously held the sword in front of him, using both hands.

"Hey, Mister, you mind telling us what's happening?" JoJo asked, a mixture of anger and fear in her voice. "All we did was ask for directions. Actually, we didn't even get to do *that* yet."

"Quiet, Girl!" Albie ordered harshly. Facing up to the men on the wall, he shouted, "We have Renegades!"

Chapter Seven

Judgment

JoJo, Marcy, and Trip were herded through the doorway by the two guards. It reminded JoJo of being on a field trip in grade school, where the teachers and parents acting as chaperones were always lining them up and pointing them in this direction or that. On those field trips, however, the kids were there to see whatever the main attraction was. Today, JoJo and her friends *were* the main attraction.

Once through the door, JoJo could see that they were actually inside a walled village of sorts. The timber wall that seemed to encircle the collection of small houses and shops had a walkway near the top, allowing posted guards to look out for approaching danger. She counted six men up there altogether, including the three that had been watching them originally. *What's so bad that they need all these guards on duty?* she wondered, returning her gaze back to ground level.

They had entered an open area that held wheelbarrows and a large collection of baskets. Hanging on the wall on either side of the doorway was an assortment of rakes, hoes, and shovels. Upon closer inspection, the door itself could actually be made to open wider, probably allowing for horse- or mule-drawn carts to go out to the fields during harvest. Men, women, and children were rapidly gathering in the spaces not taken by wheelbarrows and other farming equipment.

"You think we need to make a run for it?" Trip asked into JoJo's ear as they made their way to the middle of the clear area. She thought she caught a hint of nervousness in his voice, which had the effect of shaking her up a bit. In all the years she'd known Trip, he had never once indicated being worried about anything. Not once.

"Nah," she answered over her shoulder, trying to sound calm. "Let's see what they've got in mind before we do anything stupid." Besides, she didn't need to add, if we tried to run we'd be kissing Marcy good-bye. There's no way on God's green earth – or wherever we are – that her other friend would be able to outrun anyone who wasn't crippled. Severely crippled.

They came to a stop when the older guard halted in front of them. People had crowded into the open area all around them, but kept their distance, as if they believed these visitors to be diseased in some way. The men, women, and most of the children all wore their hair pulled back and braided, just as the guards did, revealing the single, black hoop dangling from their right ears. The youngest children wore their hair short, exposing their ears fully, the heavy obsidian earring looking massive against their necks.

"These are the Renegades?" a voice asked. It was hard to tell if it belonged to a man or woman. Albie moved off to one side, revealing a short, stout woman with her plump hands folded in front of her. Her black hair was streaked with white, and pulled back so severely that it seemed to threaten the very skin on her forehead. Like all the others, a gleaming black circle hung from her right ear lobe, lying alongside the folds of her chubby neck. She stared without warmth at the newcomers, who now stood side by side with JoJo in the middle.

"Listen, all we want –"

"Silence!" The woman cut JoJo off abruptly. "We do not suffer impertinent children in our village. We certainly do not put up with rude Renegade children. You will speak when told to, and only then."

"But…" Surprisingly, it was Marcy who started to argue. It only took one glare from the portly woman to silence her.

The woman raised an eyebrow at Trip, checking to make sure that he understood also, but he returned her look with a blank stare, as if he didn't really care. It was his way of dealing with authority figures, and he'd found it annoyed them more than arguing. Satisfied nonetheless, she continued.

"You two, lift up your hair," she ordered, looking directly at JoJo and Marcy. Having been commanded to do so once already, it didn't come as a complete surprise, and the girls did as they were told. When they both had pulled and bunched their hair up over their heads, there was a collective gasp from the gathered crowd, which had grown to thirty or forty people now.

"Where are your LifeStones?" the woman repeated the same question that the guards had asked, but it was like she had a truckload of gravel in her voice. She shifted her gaze from one to the other, including Trip, while she waited for a response.

"Ma'am," Marcy began hesitantly, not sure if she was going to be allowed to speak this time, "we don't know what LifeStones are. We're not from…"

"Nonsense! You will be taught not to lie while we hold you for the authorities. Perhaps we can instill some other manners in you as well, depending upon how long your captivity lasts. At a minimum, your heads will be shaved in accordance with the law."

"Whoa! Hold on just a minute, lady." JoJo blurted. "And don't tell me to shut up, either. We're looking for my Dad, and were hoping you people would be decent human beings and at least point us in the right direction. Instead, you treat us like we're some kind of criminals just because we're not wearing those incredibly ugly earrings. And now you think you're going to *shave our heads?* Are you nuts?"

The gasps from the crowd this time were even more pronounced, followed almost immediately by an eerie silence as everyone waited for the woman's response. JoJo was breathing heavily, her hands balled into fists.

Rather than saying anything right away, the woman looked past the three visitors, and nodded. Suddenly, three guards came forward out of the crowd. Included were the two that had escorted JoJo and her friends from the field – Albie the Old and Barney the Young. The third guard was somewhere in between the others, as far as age went, and much stronger-looking. He stopped behind Trip and placed his rough hands on the boy's upper arms, and squeezed. Hard enough to make Trip more than a little uncomfortable. Albie and Barney did the same with the girls, their grips also painful though nowhere near as firm. Marcy gave out a sharp squeal, which seemed to satisfy the young guard.

"Put them in the stocks," the roundish woman ordered, appearing to get more pleasure out of this than was called for, at least to JoJo's way of thinking. As everyone started moving toward what seemed to be the middle of the walled village, JoJo and her friends were shoved along in the same general direction. The woman in charge barked out more commands. "Send a raven to Shadowrock, informing their High Court of this breach of the law. And tell Clem to prepare his razor."

"Shadowrock? You mean 'Camelot'?" JoJo asked aloud, despite the renewed pain that Albie was inflicting as he muscled her forward. "That's the place we wanted directions to. *That's* where we need to go!"

Everyone stopped, as if her words had frozen the crowd. Slowly they turned their terrified faces right toward JoJo Mallory, who responded by sticking her chin out defiantly. Marcy wanted to shrink down to the size of an ant, if that were possible. Trip simply grinned.

"Child, no one speaks that name." The chubby woman spoke the words deliberately, as if JoJo might have trouble hearing or understanding, but not in a sympathetic way. Her face was somewhat pale now, where it had been pinkish before. "You have bitten off more than you can chew. A shaved head is the least of your worries."

JoJo continued staring right back at the woman, as she had done with authority figures so many times in the past. Ever since her mother had committed suicide. JoJo had become something of a rebel, in and out of school. While she had plenty of friends, and was fairly popular among her classmates and the other neighborhood kids, she was not a model student or citizen. Her Dad had tried everything from punishment to bribery, all with the same frustrating lack of effect. In the end, he made a rather straightforward deal with her: if JoJo would do a better job of staying out of trouble, he would make time every week to spend just with her – no work, no sisters, no other intrusions. Unbeknownst to either of them at the time, it was just what both of them had needed. Now, her father had been taken away from her.

She was going to get him back, no matter what it took. Offending someone was the least of her concerns.

"Camelot, Camelot, *Camelot!*" JoJo practically spit the last one out. The old guard released his grip and backed away from her, going several steps before he stopped uncertainly. The other two did the same, not wanting to be anywhere near the law-breaker.

Trip resisted the urge to rub the soreness out of his arms, not wanting to give his former captor the satisfaction. Marcy had no such pride when it came to physical pain, and immediately began massaging what she was certain were now bruises. Like JoJo, they curiously took in the crowd's reaction to her incantations.

"Dang, the little guy wasn't kidding about the whole 'Camelot' thing, was he?" Tripp mumbled, but still loud enough for those nearest to hear the forbidden name. Someone in the crowd fainted.

The heavy woman's face was ash-white now, her air of authority entirely replaced by a combination of stark fear and complete disbelief. Like everyone else, she retreated away from the three Renegade children. It turned out to be a wise move on her part.

Black smoke exploded in the midst of the farming equipment, sending wheelbarrows and baskets alike flying in all directions. Trip put his arms protectively around JoJo and Marcy as the three crouched in a small huddle, a large basket sailing past them. People screamed, both out of fear and from being struck by airborne farming tools.

As quickly as that, it was over, the black cloud dissipating. Standing in its place was a haggard-looking old crone of a woman, dressed completely in tattered rags the color of midnight. Her back was bent severely, as if she hadn't been able to stand up straight for decades. Thin, stringy wisps of grayish hair barely covered the top of her pink scalp and continued to the bottom of her neck. It was not tied back in the fashion of the villagers, as there was so little to it. Dangling heavily from her right ear was the same hideously black hoop that the villagers all wore. She turned ever so deliberately until she was facing JoJo and her friends. The three kids from Maine were the only other ones standing, everyone in the village now down on their knees with their faces planted in the dirt.

"Let me see," the crone said in a raspy voice. "No LifeStones, no respect, odd clothing. I'll just bet one of you was also the one to speak the unspeakable name."

Marcy started to answer, but the black-clad woman cut her off swiftly.

"No need to explain, Missy. You see, I already *know* who you are, and whom you seek. In fact, I was just visiting with him." She cackled after this last bit, apparently what was supposed to pass for laughter.

"Who *are* you?" JoJo demanded, her fists tensed at her sides.

"Oooh," the crone cackled again. Rubbing her bony hands together in front of her, she continued, "I am Creech, the youngest and wisest of the Gories. And now your worst nightmare."

Chapter Eight

A Tough Bargain

JoJo didn't know what to think. On the one hand, if the spooky-looking ancient woman in front of them had indeed seen her Dad recently, she certainly didn't want to do anything that messed up her chances to reunite with him. On the other, however, if the Leprechaun was correct about the Gories torturing her father, then this witch appeared to be pretty capable of making his life miserable.

"How is my father?" she asked, trying to keep her bravado going. "What have you and your witch-sisters done to him?"

Creech regarded her like a tigress deliberating the best way to devour its prey. "I see the pesky little imp taught you well. Unfortunately, he didn't have ample time to teach you appropriate manners."

"Oh, I've got all the manners I *need*," JoJo flipped back, shaking off Marcy's restraining hand. "I just don't give a hoot about your stupid rules. All I care about is getting my Dad back in one piece, and getting the heck out of this goofy place."

"And finding something to eat…" Marcy mumbled under her breath, earning glares from both JoJo and Trip.

"I doubt that your poor father will survive long enough to see you again," Creech sneered derisively. "He seems determined to take his little secret to the grave with him. Just like all the pathetic Free Knights we questioned before him, all resting together peacefully now in one big happy pit. Of course, your father still has quite a painful journey to complete before he joins them."

"You've got the wrong guy, for crying out loud!" JoJo pleaded. The thought of her Dad being plopped into some mass grave was almost more disturbing to her than any torture he might go through to get there. "He doesn't know anything about your… whatever it's called!"

"*Chrimeus*," Marcy offered helpfully, again under her breath.

"*Chrimeus*," JoJo repeated, continuing her argument. "He's not – we're not – even from this crazy place. He's just a carpenter from Ferry Village." Even as she said it, she wondered how much truth there was to this last statement. Was Flick right? Did Dad really have some secret past life that included living in another world altogether? That was too bizarre to wrap her head around.

Trip gazed around at the villagers still on the ground with their faces almost rubbing in the dirt. They were completely motionless, obviously too scared to even twitch. He wondered what would happen if someone sneezed. *Why hasn't the witch done anything to us if she's so mean and powerful?* he asked himself. *After all, JoJo's standing here talking back to this Creech when everyone else is afraid to breathe. She thinks we know something!*

"What if we get the Cry-moose thingy for you, but you gotta promise to quit torturing Mr. Mallory in the meantime?" Trip said aloud, startling everyone. Creech stared at him with a questioning look on her narrow face.

"He means the *Chrimeus*," Marcy clarified for the witch.

Now it was JoJo's turn to look at her hockey buddy with confusion in her eyes. Trip returned her stare with the confident air that he usually reserved for when he was on the ice. Whatever he had in mind, he wasn't being wishy-washy about it.

The Gorie was also studying the strange twelve-year old boy, looking for some clue that he was leading her on.

"You *know* where it is, Boy?" she asked, piercing him with her question as if it were a sharply pointed weapon. "Or do you perceive me to be stupid?"

Trip shrugged his shoulders, returning her stare with cold blue eyes of his own. As good a skater as he was, and as gifted a puck handler, Trip's greatest asset on the ice had always been his vision. Like the greatest players of all time, young Johnny "Triple Hat Trick" Dowling could see things on a hockey rink before they actually happened, including where the puck was going well before it got there. This was well-known among everyone who followed the crew-cut phenom, including his best friend. JoJo hoped that this vision of his extended beyond the ice.

"We know where to find it," Trip answered the witch nonchalantly, "but it's gonna take a little time. If we get there with it and JoJo's Dad is… um… not in good shape, then the deal's off. You know what I mean?"

Marcy winced as she listened to the biggest Jock at Mahoney Middle School *negotiate* with an honest-to-goodness evil witch. *It's only a matter of time,* she thought, *before we're turned into toads or incinerated into ashes.* The problem was, she didn't have anything better to put forth.

Surprisingly, Creech appeared to be considering his offer. She squinted at the boy, and then turned her attention to JoJo. Her eyes would have twinkled, had they not been swimming so deeply in darkness. JoJo shivered involuntarily, as if a winter wind had blown in.

"Unlike my sisters, I am a reasonable and enlightened soul," the witch said, seemingly amused with her own humor. She rubbed the sharp point of her chin before continuing. "I think that an accommodation can be reached."

Despite an incredible urge to say something, JoJo and her two best friends kept their mouths clamped shut. Marcy was unsure of where this was headed, but certain that they would not come out

on top. JoJo was too shaken by the mental pictures of her father

being tortured to be able to form a clear thought. Trip, meanwhile,

felt that the less they talked, the better off they were. He didn't have

to wait very long before Creech continued with her offer.

"I will give you as long as you need to locate and deliver the

Chrimeus," she said without emotion. She hesitated before

continuing. "But, just to lend a sense of urgency to your actions,

know this: your father will lose a finger every day you dither –

nothing more, nothing less. When he runs out of fingers, we will

have assumed that you are unable to deliver as promised, and our

bargain expires."

JoJo was certain that she was going to vomit. The thought of

her Dad… She shook her head violently to get rid of horrendous

vision dancing behind her eyelids. Tears were forming at the corners

of her eyes, and threatened to spill down her cheeks.

"I'm not agreeing to anything that includes hurting my Dad,"

she said finally, through gritted teeth, determined not to show weakness. Somewhere among the kneeling villagers someone squealed audibly. *Surely there would be repercussions for speaking in such a manner to one of the daughters of Pewtris Grimm himself?* seemed to be the unspoken thought.

"Then perhaps I was mistaken about your motivation," Creech replied, a flicker of anger creeping into her voice. "Let me offer you an alternative. We will leave your father unharmed, as you wish. Instead, to ensure you fully understand how little time you have, I will take a small child from a village – like this – every day that you and your friends dally."

There were shrieks from among the villagers now, although no one dared to raise their heads still. The ancient witch drank in their terror, knowing that these three young strangers would find no love among the people of Erristan – not after having just traded the well-being of some obvious criminal for the fate of their beloved children.

"What... what will you do with them?" Marcy asked with a gulp. "The children that you take?"

Creech laughed, but there was no warmth in her screechy voice. "Why, they will become servants of Shadowrock." More screams from the crowd. "After we remove their souls, of course." People actually picked their heads up as some begged the Gorie to spare their children while others yelled curses and threats at JoJo and her friends.

JoJo didn't care. These were the same people who were going to shave her head moments earlier. She wasn't about to sacrifice her Dad for this village full of misfits. Marcy looked at her in horror, the thought of little children being turned into soulless… whatever… was more than she could handle. Trip didn't look once at his lifelong friend, never worrying about which decision she would make. Instead, he stared at the bone-faced witch, vowing that he would do whatever it took to win this game.

"You've got a deal," JoJo pronounced. "Tell them to leave the front gate open."

The screams and curses started again, this time much louder, with many villagers actually rising up out of their subservient positions. Men were shaking their fists at JoJo, while women moved to cover their young children protectively.

"Silence!" Creech commanded in a voice that carried tons of authority, despite her frail appearance. "How *dare* you rise in my presence!"

Immediately, the people dropped back onto their knees, foreheads pressed firmly into the ground. Satisfied, the witch turned back to JoJo and her companions.

"One last thing, my sweet young visitors. You cannot expect to roam the countryside without the protection of the LifeStones." She held out her open hand, on which rested three of the heavy black hoops. With a flick of her wrist, she flipped the earrings toward the sixth-graders, one landing in the dirt in front of each of them. Pointing, she ordered, "Put them on!"

Chapter Nine

Friends and Enemies

JoJo bent down and picked up the shiny black ring at her feet. Marcy hesitated, then did likewise. Trip folded his arms defiantly and looked at Creech with his lips pressed together. People were always telling him what to do. Teachers, hockey coaches, his mother. Most of the time, they didn't have a clue that he was going to do whatever he wanted when all was said and done. This witch was no different, to his way of thinking.

He knew a few guys who sported ear rings, and that was fine with him. As long as no one expected him to start shoving pieces of metal – or any other material – through *his* skin. Never mind this giant black bicycle wheel.

"I don't do earrings," he said flatly. "Not my thing."

"My ears aren't pierced yet," JoJo added hopefully, weighing the humongous ebony ring in her hand.

"I don't think this will fit through my piercings," Marcy offered, holding the hideous hoop like it was a dead frog.

Creech smiled as she looked from one to the other, the skin stretched tightly over her bony face. It wasn't a smile of mirth or humor. The smile didn't reach her eyes, which were like deep black holes where souls disappear. She raised a hand and directed it toward JoJo and her friends.

The air between the witch and the middle-schoolers crackled and popped suddenly, causing JoJo, Trip and Marcy to instinctively put their hands up to shield their faces.

"That should take care of your difficulties," Creech announced. Without waiting for a response, she added in an almost sing-song voice, "Don't forget about the children."

Before they could respond, a thick cloud of smoke enveloped the ragged witch. With another explosion, the cloud dissipated, despite the lack of a breeze. Creech was gone, the place where she was standing now an empty patch of space.

"Hey, where'd she –" JoJo started to ask.

"Oh my God!" Marcy shouted, her hand on her right ear. "That *thing* – it's on my ear!" Looking at her companions, she added, "You guys, too!"

Trip and JoJo looked at her to see what the big commotion was about. Dangling from her right ear, visible through her mussed hair, was the LifeStone that had been in her hand seconds ago. The weighty black ring was threaded through her earlobe as if it had been there all along.

JoJo looked in her hand and saw that the LifeStone she'd been holding was no longer there. Reflexively, she reached up and felt her ear. *Great, I finally get my ears pierced and it's only one ear and I have to wear a basketball hoop in it.* She tugged on it and was instantly rewarded with searing pain throughout her entire body, causing her to release it immediately.

Trip stared at the spot on the ground where he'd left the ugly black ring, afraid of what he'd see. Or not see. There was nothing but the packed dirt that covered the rest of the ground. He slowly raised his right hand, feeling for what he hoped he wouldn't find.

His heart sank when his fingers touched the cold hard stone hoop. Like JoJo, he gave it a little pull. And just as had happened with her, he received a jolt that shook his whole body and caused him to immediately release the LifeStone.

"Ouch!" Marcy yelled, her hand flying away from the hideous new jewelry. As with the others, she had discovered that removing the earring was not an option. Shaking her arm to emphasize her pain, she added, "That hurt! How are we going to get these off?"

"You don't," a woman's voice answered. It was the same stout woman who had been giving all the orders before Creech arrived. She seemed to keep her distance now, either out of respect or fear, but that didn't stop her from gloating. "You children will find out now what it's like to live by rules and laws."

JoJo disregarded her with a wave of the back of her hand. She needed answers, not more problems. They still didn't know how to get from this miserable little village to Shadowrock, but at least they knew they were in the same kingdom. Hopefully, it was a small country that could be covered fairly quickly. Of course, once they got there, they still had to actually find the *Chrimeus*, assuming that the clues were on the map and they could figure them out. And now, they had these cute little ornaments firmly attached to their ears.

"What exactly do they do?" Marcy asked, her question apparently aimed at the chubby woman. "The LifeStones. Besides hurting like heck if you try to remove them, do they have an actual *purpose?*"

The woman laughed. She was joined by chuckles from the crowd, most of whom had gotten back to their feet now. The laughter was not at all good-natured, but rather more like the kind you would hear on a playground full of bullies. Without the Gorie around, the villagers were slowly rediscovering the false courage that comes from a mob.

"The LifeStones are our connection to the kingdom," the woman explained. "They let the Great Ruler know we are alive and well, and serving his purpose. In return, the LifeStones provide each and every inhabitant with protection from the evils of the world, protection against those who would otherwise bring great harm to us and the kingdom."

"Great. Sounds like a book I read called *1984*." Marcy looked at JoJo and Trip for support, but they merely shrugged their shoulders, looking as confused as the people around them. "Oh, come on – you know, Big Brother? I bet these gorgeous earrings have got some kind of GPS in them, too, right? So that your dear Great Ruler knows right where you are at any given minute, correct?"

Trip was tempted to tug at the black hoop again, but pulled his hand away at the last instant, the memory of that shooting pain still fresh in his mind. The thought of being tracked disgusted him as few things could. For as long as he could remember, he'd been able to come and go as he pleased, as long as he stayed out of trouble. His mother was too busy working and his father… well, his father had been out of the picture for long enough to say he didn't have one. Once in a while, he'd hear his mother on the phone with someone, and the subject of his father would come up, but she'd just say that they didn't have anything to do with him. The last time Trip had seen the man was probably around the time he was in kindergarten.

A few villagers ventured closer, now that the witch was gone and the smoke had cleared. Included among these were the guards who had been holding JoJo and her friends, and shoving them toward their date with the barber. They stopped short of getting too close, still somewhat unsure of what to make of these three strange children who dared speak to a Gorie, much less *bargain* with one. Nevertheless, the kids from Maine were beginning to feel crowded and anxious about getting out of this place.

Trip kept a watchful eye on those closest to them, mostly men, in addition to the fat woman. He also looked past this group, scanning for a way out. *The biggest problem with making a run for it,* he thought, *is Marcy. She'll never...* Just then, he noticed a man standing well to the rear of all the other people, almost in the shadow of a house, wearing what looked like a poncho with the hood up. It was hard to see the man's face from this far, even with Trip's acute eyesight, but the gesture was undeniable. The man was motioning with his head to a passageway behind him. When he was sure that Trip had seen him, he turned and walked in the direction that he had indicated. *What's that all about?*

Just then, a woman screamed an agonizing, heart-piercing scream. It had come from the opposite direction of where Trip had been staring. He and the girls – along with everyone else – turned to see what the commotion was about. From the sound, they probably wouldn't have been surprised if someone had suffered a horrible accident…

"She's gone!" It sounded like the same woman, although it was hard to tell because it came out as half-moan, half-screech. "My baby. They took *my baby*!"

The crowd had parted, allowing the woman to be seen. She was dressed like anyone else in the village – drab clothes that had been patched over many times. Although she was not yet thirty years old, she could have passed for twice that age. In her arms was an empty blanket, clutched to her heaving chest. She pointed a shaking finger at JoJo.

"Because of *you*! The witches took my little girl because you think your father is worth more than my Belle. Well, you're *wrong*, you evil gutter-snipe!"

JoJo backed up a step, swallowing hard at the accusation. Looking around, she could tell that everyone else in the village shared the woman's opinion of her deal with Creech. It wouldn't have been so bad if the Gorie had picked a different town for her first victim. Or had waited long enough for them to get out of this one.

"I say we put an end to this, here and now!" a man shouted, raising a rusty sword. It was the same muscular guard who had been holding Trip. Cheers and yells of support went up from the crowd. People closed in, led by the guards pointing their swords.

Marcy hugged JoJo and dropped her chin into her chest, squeezing her eyes shut. Trip stepped protectively in front of the girls, trying to determine what he could do to defend against sharp steel, no matter how rusty and chipped.

"Stop!" The deep voice was eerily familiar. The villagers did not completely obey the command, some still making their way to grab the young kids from Maine. More loudly came the second order, "Cease and desist!"

JoJo looked around before thinking to lower her line of sight. Standing between her and the guards was the same figure she'd woken up to earlier that morning.

Flick.

Chapter Ten

On the Run

The Leprechaun.

In one hand he held a gnarled wooded staff that was no more than two feet in length. He brandished the staff like a weapon, and from it blazed sparks of different colors – blue, red, green, purple. Wisps of white smoke mingled with the sparks. The people of the village shrieked and again retreated a safe distance away. Except for one, that is.

The muscular guard stood his ground, pointing his sword now at Flick.

"I'm not running from any pint-sized midget with a stick," he said gruffly, waving the sword slowly back and forth between him and the Leprechaun. "I'll chop you up and feed you to the pigs for interfering with our business."

JoJo, Marcy and Trip backed away enough to be out of range of the guard's sword, Marcy still hugging her best friend, her face buried in JoJo's shoulder and her eyes closed. JoJo and Trip, on the other hand, watched intently, curious to see how Flick was going to handle this threat.

Flick cocked an eyebrow at the guard and gave him a half-smile. "It's a shillelagh, not a stick," he corrected, as if that were the most important thing the guard had said. "And I rather doubt you'll be chopping very much with *that*."

At that instant, the guard grunted and swung his… giant feather! Trip burst out laughing as the guard waved harmlessly at Flick with what appeared to be the colorful tail feather of a peacock. The Leprechaun made no effort to get out of the way, allowing the 'weapon' to brush his arm harmlessly.

"My turn," he said, smiling and swinging the shillelagh in as wide an arc as his small stature allowed. If it had been the guard's intention to dodge, he was too slow by far.

The gnarled wooden club landed hard against the side of the man's knee with a loud *Crack!* JoJo couldn't tell if that was sound of the wood or if Flick had broken the guard's leg. Whatever the case, the man crumbled to the ground, grabbing his leg while he screamed in agony. The feather lay at his side.

Flick turned his attention to JoJo. He showed no satisfaction on his face.

"There is little time," he said grimly, repeating the same warning from earlier. "You must go."

"But where?" JoJo asked, holding up her hands helplessly. Marcy had finally let go when she heard Trip laugh. "We still don't know where we are or how to get to Cam– uh, Shadowrock."

"You will find help," Flick answered, turning his head in the direction of the poncho'd man that Trip had noticed. "But you mustn't delay. Go!"

Tapping the shillelagh once on the ground, the Leprechaun vanished into thin air. No cloud of smoke or clap of thunder – he simply disappeared. As if that posed an even greater danger, the villagers gasped and backed away even further.

"Follow me," Trip said urgently, not waiting for his companions to say anything. He wanted to take advantage of these people being stunned by Flick's antics, afraid that it would wear off before long, and they would be hard to deal with again. Walking quickly toward the passageway that the man had indicated, Trip looked once over his shoulder to make sure the girls were with him.

JoJo had no trouble keeping up, and Marcy was managing well enough, even though it required that she run every few steps to keep from falling behind. The villagers in their path moved to the sides, like Moses parting the Red Sea. In their eyes was a mixture of fear and awe. It was only a matter of time before some of that would be replaced with anger, but for now no one wanted anything to do with these bizarre children who brought forth witches and Leprechauns.

"Where are we going?" JoJo asked softly as they arrived at the corner of the house where the strange man had been standing.

Trip looked around for the man with the hooded poncho, but he was nowhere to be seen. A few of the villagers seemed to be coming out of their trance-like daze, grumbling about disappearing babies and bad mojo. It was time to get out of town.

"This way," Trip answered, taking off again, this time down the shadowed passageway that the man had indicated. At least, Trip was pretty sure that that's what he had done.

Marcy was already struggling to keep up as Trip had picked up speed. It wasn't that he was in a dead sprint – she would have been left way behind if that had been the case – but he wasn't wasting any time, either. The passageway that he'd chosen wound between houses, bending this was and that. Every now and then, they had to jump over puddles of nasty-looking water that looked to be mixed with garbage. Whatever it was, it gave off a rank smell like a dumpster. Marcy would be all too happy when they were out of this winding alley. *And it would be nice,* she thought miserably, *if would could go somewhere without having to run.*

She got a chance to catch her breath when she almost ran into Trip and JoJo, who had suddenly stopped in front of her. The narrow passageway had come to an end between the corners of two small houses. Peeking around one of the corners, they could see a large, open gate in the wall not far away. There was a single guard on the walkway above, but none on the ground that they could see. A dirt road led through the gate into the village. The guard's attention was on something or someone outside the gate, his back turned for the moment, and his spear leaning against one shoulder.

"Ok, we're going to have to get up to that gate quickly, but without making any noise," Trip whispered, "and then we need to run. Are you guys up for that?"

"We're good," JoJo answered for both of the girls, although everybody knew that the question was meant for Marcy, who just pressed her lips together tightly and nodded. "At least, that guard doesn't have a bow-and-arrow."

"Let's go," Trip said, anxious to be away from the unfriendly surroundings. He led them around the corner and past the end of the house. The closer to the wall that they stayed, the harder it would be for the guard overhead to spot them, blocked as he was by the walkway.

Just as they neared the gate's nearest door, which opened inward and blocked their view of the outside somewhat, they heard voices from outside the gate. Trip signaled them to freeze, which Marcy didn't do until she caught up completely, earning an annoyed scowl from him. One of the voices belonged to a man, the other to a woman, and they appeared to be arguing about something. The proper way to hitch a horse or some such thing, from the sounds of it. Trip held the girls back with a wave of his hand while taking a peek past the edge of the gate door. He pulled back immediately.

"What's up?" JoJo asked, wanting to look past Trip, but he barred her with his arm.

"There's another guard out there, and some lady with a horse-cart or whatever they call it. I know I can make it past them with no problem, and probably JoJo, too but..." He looked at Marcy as the sentence hung in the air unfinished.

"I'll try, I promise." It came out as a hoarse whisper as she looked up at JoJo and Trip with watery eyes. "I'm just not used to all this running."

"Maybe you could give the guard a little hip-check on the way by, Trip," JoJo suggested, hopefully. "You know, buy Marcy and me a little more time."

It wasn't the style of hockey that Trip was known for. He was a skater, a veritable Rembrandt on the ice, a thing of beauty in a rough, violent game. *But heck*, he thought, *even Bobby Orr and Wayne Gretzky had to throw their weight around every now and then, just to keep everyone honest.* And it wasn't as if he didn't know how. He had simply decided long ago that he wasn't going to be the goon type of hockey player who forgot what the object of the game was.

"Okay," he said after visualizing the whole thing in his head, "you two run like hell as soon as I say 'go!', and stay on my right side." He patted his right hip for emphasis. "Just stay on the dirt road and keep running until I tell you to stop."

Marcy took a deep breath and blew it out, clenched her fists and actually began running in place to help get herself ready. Neither JoJo nor Trip said anything. He looked past the gate door once again. There was nothing particularly dangerous-looking about this guard, other than the fact that he was about a head taller and twice as heavy as Trip. And he was holding a long spear with a pointy metal tip. The only good thing was that he seemed to be totally engrossed in his conversation with the lady.

"Go!" Trip said as he bolted around the edge of the door and headed straight for the guard. JoJo wasted no time, digging her boots into the dirt and pumping her arms, staying on Trip's right flank. Marcy gritted her teeth and followed, determined not to hold them up. She tried not to focus on how fast Trip had blazed ahead of them.

The guard never saw him coming, but the woman with the horse-cart did. Rather than yell or otherwise react to the oncoming youth, she continued to draw the guard's attention. As a result, Trip was able to knock the unsuspecting guard completely off his feet. From up on the wall, they heard the other guard shout a late warning.

JoJo was already heading down the dirt road that led out of the village, trees on one side and an open field on the other. She looked back to check on the others, and was not surprised to find Trip about to pass her, having recovered from planting the vicious check on the guard. Marcy was about twenty feet behind, and not catching up. The guard was back on his feet and angry, embarrassed by what had happened but determined to make someone pay. It was easy for him to decide who that would be.

Despite her best efforts, Marcy knew she wasn't running fast enough. Looking over her shoulder for at least the tenth time, she screamed as the hand belonging to the guard reached for her neck.

She braced for the touch and tried not to think of what would follow.

Chapter Eleven

The Free Knight

JoJo and 'the Jock' were way down the dirt road from her, not cursed with Marcy's turtle-like slowness. She wished they'd stop and wait for her, but she also knew that they couldn't keep doing that. It was a case of hating them for being fast as much as hating herself for being so incredibly slow.

Marcy felt like she was running in a giant bowl of Jell-O. No matter how hard she tried, she couldn't make her legs propel her any faster than this pathetically slow pace. On top of that, she was already exhausted, ready to just give up and collapse to the ground where she could catch her breath again and make all the pain go away. While she could figuratively run circles around everyone else in the classroom, she stunk at the physical version of running. What she couldn't understand was why that guard's hand had not clamped around her throat by now. It had been right there the last time she dared to look, and there was no way that she had suddenly started running faster than him, was there?

Chancing a peek, she turned her head and tensed, expecting… Nothing. The hand wasn't there. Nor was the guard that it belonged to. She thought she saw a lump of clothing on the side of the road, but she couldn't be sure if that was the guard. *Who cares?* she thought to herself, elated. Returning her attention to her companions ahead, she ran with actual enthusiasm to catch up.

"What happened?" JoJo asked when they were all together again, Marcy bent over with her hands on her knees and breathing hard. "You did great, Marce!"

"You really did," Trip added, a genuine look of respect on his face. He gingerly rubbed the hip that he'd used on the guard. "That was not an easy run, by any stretch."

Marcy stood up, able to breathe normally again, although her face was still red from the exertion. "I don't know. One minute the guard was about to grab me, and the next thing you know he's not there. I know I didn't outrun him, so I can't tell you *what* happened.

Maybe Flick popped out of nowhere and did some kind of Leprechaun magic to him?"

They started walking, now that Marcy was mostly recovered, each of them looking back toward the village to see if they were being chased. With the woods on one side, it would be easy enough to duck away among the trees if they had to, but it made sense to stay on the road as much as they could. Well, it made sense if they knew where they were going, and if the road happened to take them in the right direction…

While the forest offered them a refuge to escape into, they had not given any thought to the possibility that someone might come *out of* the same wooded area at them. Which is exactly why they all jumped when a man appeared suddenly from among the trees next to them.

"Hello." It was the second time that day that someone had scared the bejeebers out of JoJo with just that simple greeting.

This time, however, the greeter was a full-grown man, as big as her Dad and rugged-looking like some of the men from her neighborhood back home. He wore a brown cloak that was fastened in the front with a couple of oblong wooden buttons. The cloak also had a hood that covered the man's head and hid part of his face in shadow.

"You're the guy from back in the village, aren't you?" Trip asked, pointing at the man. "The one who told us how to get out of there?"

"I am," the man answered, his voice gravelly. He sounded like someone none of them would ever want to upset.

"Did you do something to that guard that was chasing me?" Marcy asked, waving a hand in the direction of the village.

"I did." They waited for him to elaborate, but apparently that wasn't going to happen without more questioning. Instead, JoJo went in a different direction.

"Are you the help that Flick talked about?"

The man smiled, his scruffy beard moving to the sides, and it caught the children off-guard. Up until now, they would have thought him incapable of smiling, or at least unwilling. He pulled the hood down, revealing salt-and-pepper hair that came down over his ears. He was not wearing one of the black LifeStones, which prompted JoJo to reach up and feel for hers. Unfortunately, it was still there.

"My name is Caleb. I am a Free Knight, one of the very last in existence. I offer you my sword, my service, and – if need be – my life."

JoJo took a step back from the man. This was like something out of the movies. In real life, no one said things like that. At least, no one she'd ever met before. She looked at her friends, first Marcy and then Trip, to see if they thought this was as bizarre as she did. Judging by their expressions, they were either just as shocked as JoJo or thought the whole thing was pretty cool. She looked the Free Knight up and down, taking in his rough clothing that was visible under the open cloak: a loose gray shirt, snug dark trousers tucked into worn calf-high boots, and a sheathed sword hanging from its wide black belt. On his hands were large, dark leather gloves.

"I don't get it," she finally said, returning her eyes to his face. "I mean, why would you want to help us? You don't even know us or what we're after."

"The Leprechaun fella could've told him," Trip suggested out of the side of his mouth while still facing Caleb. "Just sayin'."

Marcy was still nervously looking back toward the village, expecting to see an angry mob coming down the dirt road at any minute. She was still trying to understand how this Free Knight – whatever that was – had dispatched the owner of the hand that had been about to grab her, and then still gotten around in front of them. Not that she was complaining, of course.

"The danger is not from the village," Caleb said, noticing Marcy's nervousness. Facing JoJo once again, he continued, "It is true that the Free Knights ally ourselves with all of the Pure Folk – whether they be Leprechauns, Fairies, or others – who seek the common goal of removing the shadow from our existence. Indeed, there are too few Knights to hope to accomplish that objective alone. Even at our peak, we were no match for Pewtris Grimm and his dark minions, and we are but a tiny morsel of that now. Our only hope is what you also seek."

"To free my Dad from the witches?" JoJo replied. "Because that's the only thing we're after. We didn't come here to start anything with these people or join up in anyone's revolution or whatever you guys are doing."

The smile was gone from the Free Knight's bearded face, replaced once again by the hardened seriousness that usually resided there. It was not anger, but it also told JoJo and her friends that this man did not often joke around. Surprising them, he began to pull off one of his gloves. *What's this all about,* JoJo wondered silently. *I hope he's not going to slap me with that thing, like a challenge or something.* When he had the glove completely off, he extended his bare fist toward her. On his middle finger was a plain gold ring with a smooth bulging section where a gemstone might have gone. JoJo gulped.

"Do you recognize this ring?" Caleb asked her in a kind but demanding tone. His face said that he already knew the answer.

"How could she possibly…?" Marcy interrupted. "I mean, that's a pretty common-looking ring." She looked at JoJo, who was staring wordlessly at the Knight's hand.

"Does it open?" she asked finally, locking eyes with Caleb.

"What's going on?" Trip asked, every bit as confused as Marcy.

Reaching over with his gloved hand, Caleb twisted the ring. The smooth dome swiveled open, revealing a symbol of some kind underneath. Marcy and Trip strained their necks to get a better look, but JoJo merely glanced down briefly, just long enough to confirm what she already knew. Rather than saying anything, she reached into her shirt from the neckline and withdrew a thin metal chain. Hanging from the chain was a plain gold ring. She held it firmly while twisting it with her other hand, opening the bulging smooth center section. When she pulled her hand away, they could all see what was inside – the exact same symbol that pointed from the Free Knight's fist.

A sword on a star.

"What…? How come you guys have the same…?" Marcy was at an unusual loss for words. "JoJo, there's obviously something you're not telling us. Or at least, not telling me. I don't know how much Mister Hockey Puck here knows, but… what's this all about?"

Trip wasn't sure whether he was being insulted or honored as he considered what Marcy had just called him. Like her, he was trying to figure out what was going on, and with the same lack of success. He shrugged her off, and concentrated on JoJo, who was looking almost guilty.

"I found this ring in my Dad's room when we were searching for clues like Flick told us to do," she explained. "I'd never seen it before. At first, I thought it was his old wedding band, but then for some reason, I gave it a little twist and it opened. I figured it was just something to keep reminding me of Dad while we're looking for him, so I put it on a chain. I didn't think it was any big deal. I still don't have any idea of what it means."

"That symbol represents the fight against darkness, and is what identifies a Knight from an impostor," Caleb answered solemnly. "We do not show the symbol openly because… well, let's just say that the current ruler of Erristan is not very fond of the Free Knights. This confirms what the Leprechaun told me about you.

"Your father is a Free Knight."

Chapter Twelve

The Chimeus

JoJo was speechless. Her brain was spinning as she tried to grasp what Caleb had just told them, and what it really meant. *How could Dad possibly be a Free Knight in* this *world and be our Dad in the other... our world? It doesn't make any sense.* She wasn't even sure of what question to ask next, or if she wanted to ask any more questions, for that matter. The others were staring at her, concern on the faces of her friends and a kind of quiet solidness from Caleb.

"JoJo, are you okay?" she heard Marcy asking, as if through a fog bank.

Could this be why Dad is so interested in history? Our history? Because it's not what he grew up with? So he's trying like heck to catch up on whatever's happened in our world since whenever because it's different than... Oh my god! This can't be happening. He's just a carpenter from Ferry Village, for crying out loud! Isn't he?

"Hey, kiddo – you in there?" Trip waved a hand in front of JoJo's face, but it took a few seconds to register, snapping her out of what looked like a trance. "You going to be all right?"

JoJo bit her bottom lip the way she always did when making a tough decision. This was a little different, however, than which shirt to wear with which pants, or whether A was a better selection than C on a multiple-choice math test. Her whole existence was being called into question, and she felt like she needed – no, *deserved* – answers. But that was going to have to wait. Free Knight or simple carpenter, whatever Dad was couldn't be answered until and unless they got him safely away from the Gories.

"What's the *Chrimeus*, Caleb?" she said, coming out of her silence. As she tried to organize her thoughts about rescuing her father, the question that had been residing deep in the back of her mind finally came to the surface. "I mean, I get that it's magic and all, but it seems like there's other magic around, so what's really so stinking important about this thing?"

The Free Knight did not appear to be surprised by her question. He didn't seem like the type who was easily surprised by anything, at least not as far as JoJo could tell. Caleb looked down at her like a kind but stern uncle, about to explain something uncomfortable.

"You speak easily of places and people and things that the inhabitants of this land would never utter," he began, grinning ever so slightly. "Erristan has been under Pewtris Grimm's heel for so many centuries that people have come to accept it as the way life should be. The *Chrimeus* is the key to changing that, to restoring the land to the way it was in the days of King Arthur and Camelot…"

"Don't you have to say 'Shadowrock'?" Marcy interrupted, looking over her shoulder to see if something bad happened.

"Only if you buy into the fear and control of Grimm and his witch-spawn. I am a Free Knight, and by definition, I do not acknowledge their rule. In fact, the Free Knights collectively and individually resist the poisonous reign of Pewtris Grimm, few though we may be. In turn, the Gories send their hounds – the Black Wind – out to search for me and the last of my brothers, hunting us like animals to be brought back to their torture chambers. There, they seek to extract any information that might assist in the extermination of the Free Knights, including the identities and locations of the remaining Knights. Mostly, however, Grimm is after the *Chrimeus*."

"Why don't you guys just make more Free Knights?" Trip asked, mesmerized by the story thus far. "I mean, when hockey players retire they're always being replaced by young guys coming up through the system. You know, like the junior leagues and college? And below them is high school and youth leagues and all the way down to Pee Wees. Why couldn't you do something like that?"

Caleb regarded Trip silently, as if he were sizing him up. Trip was used to people looking at him like this, however, so it didn't rattle him one bit. Given the chance, he always ended up earning their respect once he got out on the ice. He wasn't cocky about it, just confident.

"You make a good point. I have no idea what 'hockey' is, or some of the other things you speak of, but I understand the thrust of your question. The simple answer is that while we can train young men in the arts of being a knight, we cannot convey the special attributes that come with being a Free Knight. That is where the *Chrimeus* comes in."

"I don't get it," Marcy said, scratching her head uncharacteristically. "What kind of attributes are you talking about – bravery, invisibility, x-ray vision? You and Mister Mallory don't seem all that different than anyone else, at least not as far as I can tell." She looked at JoJo for support, especially the part about her father, and received a shrug in response.

"I am afraid that I am not free to divulge what your question seeks, young lady. Part of the reason for this is your own safety, but the primary reason is to safeguard the secrets of the *Chrimeus*. What you do not know cannot be tortured out of you."

JoJo swallowed hard. She had always considered herself to be a fairly tough kid, in that she thought she handled pain a lot better than most kids her age – boy or girl. She didn't pitch a fit whenever she got a splinter or faint at the sight of blood. Once, while horsing around a little too roughly with her father and sisters, her pinky finger had become dislocated, popping out of joint at an odd angle. Her older sisters screamed bloody murder at the sight, but Dad had calmly reset the finger without any fuss. He'd even grinned a bit as he quickly and expertly pulled and pushed to get everything back where it belonged. But that wasn't torture. Not even close. The pictures that whizzed through her mind included *all* of her fingers being pulled out of joint one at a time. She shook her head to clear the nightmare away, and noticed that her heart had been pounding a good bit faster than normal.

She took a deep breath, and then blew it out slowly.

"Look, whatever you can't tell us is fine," JoJo said, looking up at Caleb, "as long as you can help us get to Camelot quickly. And it wouldn't hurt if you could also tell us how to get rid of these gigantic earrings, since I noticed you're not wearing one."

Trip and Marcy both reached up to confirm that their ugly black hoops were still affixed to their ear lobes. As soon as their fingers made contact with the unwanted objects, they each made disappointed faces, as if they had been wishing that the LifeStones had magically disappeared.

"I shall do much more than that," Caleb answered. "But first, I would know your names. I have given you mine."

"Oh, I'm sorry. I'm JoJo, and this is Marcy and Trip." She gestured with her hands at each introduction, in case the Free Knight mistakenly assigned the names to the wrong people. Her friends nodded their heads and mumbled something along the lines of 'Hey' or 'Nice to meet you', and then started looking at the ground and shuffling their feet uncomfortably. Marcy was much more at ease around adults than she was kids her own age, but something about Caleb's imposing presence made her feel small and meek. Trip was a hockey phenom, not a social one.

"Very pleased, indeed, to be at your service," Caleb said when it appeared that no one would be adding anything to the introductions. "First things first – we need to get you to Beglis to remove those cursed shackles from your ears."

"Beglis?" Trip asked. "What's a Beglis?"

Caleb went on to explain that Beglis was, in fact, an old warlock who operated in secrecy from his lair deep in the forest. Most people never ventured far enough into the woods to confirm his existence because tales of stray travelers being turned into all sorts of weird creatures were enough to keep all but the bravest away. Since only a few knew the exact location of Beglis' den, the majority of people avoided the forest altogether. When travel through the woods was absolutely necessary, wary travelers opted to stay on one of the few roads available amongst the trees.

The Free Knights and Beglis weren't exactly friends, but they did share a common enemy in Pewtris Grimm. This enmity was the basis for an unlikely alliance between a group whose entire existence was based on honor and the restoration of the kingdom and a grumpy wizard who could care less about anyone but himself. In addition to wiping out the Free Knights, however, Grimm and his witch-daughters were also committed to extinguishing any magical beings outside of Shadowrock. This included the enchanted Pure Folk, as well as rogue wizards, sorcerers, or even apothecaries whose only offense was to mix potions, usually for healing the sick. As far as Beglis was concerned, the Free Knights were the last layer of protection between him and the hunting parties of the Gories.

Caleb explained that the tricky part was going to be getting JoJo and her friends close enough without revealing the location of Beglis' lair. The LifeStones acted as a kind of tracking device – a primitive but effective GPS – that told Creech and her witch-sisters the exact whereabouts of their wearers. The warlock would certainly not agree to allowing these strange children to lead the Black Wind right to his front door, no matter how urgent their quest. Caleb would have to ride ahead, meet with Beglis, and convince him to meet at an agreed-upon spot in the forest. It would be up to JoJo, Marcy, and Trip to get to that spot, quickly and without commotion.

"How do we find it?" Marcy asked when Caleb finished. "I mean, it's not like we have a map, and I doubt there's going to be a bright neon sign in the middle of the woods to tell us when we get there."

"It will not be difficult to find," he answered, unsmiling. "You will stay on the forest road until you come to an arch formed by two massive oaks on either side of the road. Turn into the woods directly on the right, and proceed until you arrive at a large, solitary boulder among the trees. He will meet you there."

"What about you?" JoJo asked, suddenly terrified at the idea of meeting the warlock without Caleb present. "Aren't you going to be there, too?"

"There is not time. I must ride ahead to prepare the way. Rest assured, we will meet again."

"When? Where?" JoJo gulped.

"At the gates of Camelot."

Chapter Thirteen

The Road Less Traveled

They had been walking nonstop for the past couple of hours.

In the distance, JoJo thought she heard low rumblings of thunder.

Oh great, she thought. *That's all we need is for the sky to open up*

and soak us. It's not enough that we have to walk across half this

country without a real meal in our stomachs, listening to Marcy

moaning and groaning every few steps. Now we actually get a

chance to be miserable!

Caleb had given them instructions before leaving them.

Primarily, he told them to continue along the dirt road that they'd

been on until they ran into the forest road. He said that they

wouldn't have any problem identifying the point where the forest

road split off into the woods, and he was right. Either side of the

beginning of the forest road was marked with huge malicious-

looking dead trees, looming like giant guards, even though it was hardly necessary. Only the foolish would voluntarily enter the realm

of the trees.

The Free Knight had also provided them with dried biscuits,

wrinkled apples, and animal skins filled with water before parting

ways. It wasn't much, to say the least, but it satisfied Marcy's

immediate hunger, which meant that JoJo and Trip didn't have to

listen to those complaints for a little while. The other provision that

Caleb had given them was something to defend themselves with.

Sort of. Not like swords or bows-and-arrows or any kind of real

weapons. He gave them each a pouch full of round, smooth walnut-

sized stones, along with a Y-shaped piece of wood a little bigger

than a ping-pong paddle. A narrow strip of stretchy material – most

likely the intestine of some medium-sized animal – connected the

top ends of the Y, with a larger rectangular piece of leather located

about halfway along the strip. Sling-shots. For some reason, Marcy

had been excited about getting the primitive weapons. JoJo and Trip

stuck the things in their back pockets and tied the pouches to front

belt loops on their pants.

"How much further before we get there?" Marcy asked for at least the twentieth time. "If it's not soon, we're going to get wet."

"I hope that's the worst of our problems," JoJo replied, hunching her shoulders. "This place gives me the creeps."

The forest road had taken them into the darkness of the woods, even though it was just past midday. With the gathering rainclouds, it was only going to get even darker soon. The only good news was that they didn't feel the need to watch for other travelers like they did on the main road. Caleb had told them to keep out of sight as much as possible, which meant ducking into the trees and bushes every time they heard the hoof beats of approaching horses. That had happened four times in the first hour alone, causing them to dive past tree trunks and through the thick underbrush in search of safe hiding places. Normal travelers probably wouldn't pose too much trouble, he had explained, but there were always bandits and other ruffians to consider. Worst of all, they needed to avoid the Black Wind at all costs.

Turning onto the forest road had virtually eliminated the threat of running into anyone, with the exception of the Black Wind. The Gories routinely sent patrols of their henchmen through the woods, looking for those who were hiding from the witches and Pewtris Grimm. Lawbreakers like the Free Knights and the Pure Folk. And rogue wizards and sorcerers. These Black Wind patrols generally consisted of one or two Trackers along with four or five Assassins, all under the command of a Half-lock – a sort of dark, partial warlock created by the Gories to be able to channel the lower levels of black magic. According to Caleb, Half-locks could hold their own with many of the Pure Folk, and defeat some of the enchanted beings outright. Even against a full warlock, these twisted creations were capable of causing no small amount of havoc. Without the Half-locks to lead them, the Trackers and Assassins that comprised the Black Wind patrols would be extremely hesitant about chasing anything hidden in the forest. JoJo hoped that she and her friends didn't have to find out any more about the Black Wind or Half-locks than what Caleb had already described.

The sound of horses coming up from behind them told her otherwise. It was joined a few seconds later by the noise of rainfall, lightly for the first couple of pitter-patters, and then followed immediately by the heavy roar of a downpour. Trip grabbed the girls and pulled them off the road, wet branches slapping their faces as they struggled through the thick growth at the base of the trees. Just before ducking out of sight, Trip glanced toward the direction of the hoof beats. His heart rose up into his throat as he could just make out the dark shapes pounding through the torrential rain. There were at least half a dozen of them, black cloaks flapping above their charging mounts, mud and dirty water flying up all around the massive hooves. Straight at him.

He wasn't sure if they'd spotted him as he disappeared through the curtain of shrubbery. The girls had stopped and crouched down, hoping to be less noticeable by being completely still. Trip had hoped that they'd gone a bit further before trying to conceal themselves, but he wasn't about to tell them to start moving again right now. Stooping down low, he joined them and motioned with his finger to his lips that they should not make a peep. Despite the near-deafening fall of the rain through the trees, they could hear the horses coming.

Marcy sneezed. Twice. Not real loudly, but they weren't sounds that belonged to the forest. Still, with the noise of the rain and their own splashing through puddles, the horses should have continued right on by their hiding place. Except that one of the Trackers pulled up short at the unexpected and out-of-place sound.

How in the world did he hear that? Trip thought to himself when the horse stopped less than ten feet from where he was squatting in the bushes. *What is* wrong *with that girl? Why couldn't she just... OH HECK!"*

The rider had jumped down from his horse, his black boots sucking through the muddy trail. He was walking straight toward their hiding spot. The other horses had turned around by now, and were gathering nearby.

"What do you see, Tracker?" a hoarse voice asked from atop one of the horses.

"Broken branches, Master," the man on the ground answered. Much closer and Trip would be able to reach out and touch him. Or vice-versa. "These are freshly broken. Whatever or whoever did this cannot be far away."

"Perhaps a deer?" the hoarse question pierced the rain easily.

"No, Master. There would be prints, and a deer would choose a path of less resistance rather than barreling through such dense brush. This was done by a person, probably a short one and most likely more than one."

"Such as those that we were instructed to keep an eye on," the hoarse voice responded. Trip was distracted by the Half-lock's voice, and almost didn't see the Tracker lunging toward him.

"Go!" he yelled to JoJo and Marcy, lifting them by their elbows and shoving them away from the road and the Black Wind. He felt a large hand on his shoulder just as he moved to follow the girls. Rather than resist, Trip relaxed his body and slumped to the ground. Reflexively, the Tracker loosened his grip, figuring that he had his prey under control. He was wrong.

Trip quickly rolled forward once before bouncing back up to his feet. In an instant, he was off and running, thrashing his way through the bushes and catching up with JoJo and Marcy in short order. They could hear the shouts behind them, and the noise of the Tracker making his way through the underbrush. It wasn't long before he was joined by others from the patrol. There were no unhindered paths to take, and JoJo was struggling to clear a way for them through the dense growth. Marcy pulled to one side suddenly and turned to face their pursuers.

"What are you *doing*?" Trip demanded, trying to pull her back. The Tracker was only four or five steps away.

"Watch out," Marcy replied, pulling back with one hand while extending the other forward. She was holding the sling-shot and had a stone loaded and drawn. Just in time, Trip ducked to the side.

The stone whizzed past his head and struck the Tracker squarely in the center of the astounded man's forehead, dropping him in his tracks. The next man was a good forty feet further back, but Marcy wasted no time re-loading and taking aim. When she released the stone, she watched with confidence as it shot through the air with the precision of a laser, never wavering from its course, until it also struck its target just above the bridge of the Assassin's nose. Trip stared in disbelief.

"Oh, close your mouth, will you?" Marcy said, annoyed. "You're not the only one who can hit the target, you know?" With that, she turned and began running to catch up with JoJo, who had been too busy trailblazing to watch the marksmanship demonstration. She was only a little way ahead of them, so it didn't take long to catch up, even for Marcy.

Trip took one more look back before following. He could hear one or two more men beating their way through the brush, but he couldn't see them. Neither of the two that Marcy had downed had gotten back to their feet, so Trip and the girls had a little breathing space. For now. And all because of Marcy and her sling-shot. *Are you kidding me?* he asked himself. *What's next – am I going to be able to do Algebra or something?*

Chapter Fourteen

No Compass

"How did you *do* that?" Trip asked when they finally came to a stop.

"Shhh!" JoJo cut him off sharply. No one said anything for a full sixty seconds as they strained to listen for anyone chasing them. Tromping through the wet underbrush had kept them from being able to hear all but the loudest noises, so the Black Wind could have been fairly close without their even realizing it. They had clawed and scrambled their way for what seemed like hours, but was actually closer to forty minutes, before feeling safe enough to catch their breaths.

"JoJo, you should've seen it... um, her... well, the thing..." Trip continued where he'd left off, imitating Marcy's use of the sling-shot.

"Don't hurt yourself," Marcy said with a snarky grin. She was glad to finally get some respect from the Jock, even if it was for doing something Jock-like herself. This was hardly the same as knowing the difference between radium and radius, she admitted after a moment's thought, but it was about the most she could expect.

"What happened?" JoJo asked, completely baffled by this strange exchange between her opposite best friends. "What in the world did I miss?"

Trip described how Marcy had eliminated their two closest pursuers with incredible precision using her sling-shot. Of course, he put everything in hockey terms whenever he could, as it made it easier when relating the story. Marcy's shots were likened to the pucks that Trip had fired at goals, only a thousand times more accurate. He couldn't stop gushing over the exact placement of the stones on the foreheads of the men chasing them. When JoJo looked at Marcy for an explanation, her geeky friend shrugged her shoulders.

"My mom's an engineer. We did a science project about force and trajectory and aerodynamics, and we decided to use a sling-shot to demonstrate how all of these aspects interacted. Anyway, it didn't win, but it was a lot of fun. I learned to shoot one of these pretty well by the time it was all over." She held her sling-shot up like it was no more dangerous than a pencil.

"Geez, I did my science project on peanut butter and jelly sandwiches," JoJo said, amazed by what she'd just heard. "At the time, I thought it was pretty neat, but now I need to talk to Dad about how lame it was compared to yours."

Marcy smiled and looked at Trip. "How about you? What did you do for your science project?" This was clearly her comfort zone, her hockey rink.

"I don't remember," Trip mumbled, looking away. "Nothing important, I guess. Let's get moving before those guys get a chance to catch up."

It was quite obvious that he didn't want to discuss anything to do with his own school work. Marcy had no idea of how hard

Trip struggled to keep up academically. To her, it was just a matter of cracking open a few books and soaking up whatever was in them. She couldn't comprehend how anyone could actually have trouble with learning if they were really trying. In her book, it was especially true of Jocks, who simply chose sports over studying. To Marcy's way of thinking, athletics came naturally to those kids while the Geeks had to work hard at everything. In essence, Jocks were simply lazy and she had no sympathy for their academic battles.

"Do you think it's safe to go back toward the forest road?" JoJo asked, not really directing her question at one or the other. "I mean, we're never going to find this Beglis guy otherwise."

"Yeah, I want to get rid of this stupid earring as soon as I can," Trip answered, reaching up but careful not to tug on the shiny black hoop. "I don't know about heading where those guys might be looking for us, though. Seems to me that they're just going to cruise up and down that road, waiting for us to show our faces again."

"Well, we're never going to find some big boulder in the middle of these woods just by wandering around." JoJo looked from one side to the other, just in case the giant rock was right there after all. "I'm not even sure which way it is back to the road."

The thickness of the underbrush was indeed enough to disorient them. As they had made their way through the dense bushes and tightly packed trees their concerns had been the Black Wind behind them and the whipping branches that constantly threatened to slap their faces. Fear had driven them, and adrenaline had sustained them, pushing them further away from the only lifeline that they had in the dismal forest. Now, simply returning to the forest road was itself a daunting challenge.

"I think I can get us there," Trip said, staring back at the way they'd come. Without waiting for a response, he started walking. "Follow me."

Marcy and JoJo exchanged looks. Trip was not really the type to take the lead in anything that didn't involve a pair of skates and a hockey stick. While Marcy had very little experience around him, she'd already figured out that this Jock generally preferred to let others do all the leading. JoJo knew Trip better than anyone else on the planet, and quickly came to the realization that her buddy had something else on his mind. Something that was bothering him enough to take him out of character like this. *It's probably that stuff about the science project,* she told herself. *He's just embarrassed because his project didn't turn out too well, and he almost ended up flunking because of it. Marcy's over here talking about 'not winning' and her project being 'a lot of fun', and poor Trip's thinking it was the worst experience of his life. I've got to remember to steer her away from bringing up stuff like that.*

They fought their way back through combative branches, winding around trees and bushes that were too thick. Although the rain had mostly stopped, everything was still wet and drops fell on them whenever a breeze blew through the leaves overhead. Their clothes were pretty much soaked through which, along with the cooler temperature, combined to make the three companions fairly miserable. Nevertheless, they still had to attempt to keep the noise of their passage down as much as possible, just in case the bad guys were within earshot.

At first, Trip led them in generally the correct direction, deviating slightly in a manner that would have them intersect the forest road a bit further along than where they had exited it. With each twist and turn demanded by obstacles in his path, however, he was unknowingly guided away from that destination, instead taking up a heading that ran parallel to the road. They continued like this for a while, stopping occasionally to listen for any unwanted company.

"Do you think we're headed in the right direction?" JoJo whispered to Trip during one of the stops. "I mean, we've been going at it for quite a while, and I'd have thought we would run into the road by now, you know?"

He pressed his lips together, and she could tell that he was in serious thought. Making a sour face, he answered, "I don't know, JoJo. I was thinking that we'd hit that road a while ago, too. Now I'm worried that we might be going the wrong way, but I don't want to turn and end up making it worse. Maybe you better ask the brainiac what she thinks."

The way he said it made JoJo wince. Not because she was worried that Marcy heard him, but because she could hear the hurt in his voice. "She's no better at this than you are," she said to him reassuringly before turning. "Marcy –"

Hoof beats splashed in the mud and water nearby, cutting her off. As if by reflex, all three of them crouched down next to a massive tree trunk, worried that they might be seen if they remained standing. The horse and its rider sounded as if they were no more than twenty feet away, even though there was no road visible from where they huddled. The thickness of the undergrowth had served to both obscure their objective from their sight and conceal them from the Black Wind. Soon, more sloshy pounding announced the arrival of other horses. They all seemed to be gathering right here.

Trip held his finger to his lips, unnecessarily signaling the girls to keep quiet. *Like I was going to belt out a song right about now,* Marcy thought derisively. *Sheesh, this guy sure does like being the boss.*

"What have you found?" They recognized the hoarse voice from earlier.

"Not a trace, Master. They have not returned to the road. Would you have us dismount and track them among the trees?"

"Yes, and try to protect yourself better this time," the hoarse voice sneered in response. "We will leave our horses here, since it's an easy spot to identify. It doesn't take a Tracker to find an archway made of giant oak trees."

Chapter Fifteen

No Way Out

Arch? Big oak trees? Marcy, Trip and JoJo looked at one another with wide-eyed surprise, and then stared at the massive tree trunk next to them. JoJo pointed a finger at it, mouthing the words, *Is this oak?* Marcy nodded her head emphatically up and down.

They listened intently, trying to determine what the Black Wind patrol was doing. *We gotta get out of here!* the voice inside JoJo's head screamed as she bit her lip. Wordlessly, she tapped Trip on the shoulder. When she had his and Marcy's attention, she signaled that they needed to get moving, indicating the direction with her hand. According to their instructions from Caleb, they were to turn directly to the right off the forest road when they came to the oaken archway, and proceed in a straight line until they arrived at the lone boulder, which they supposedly couldn't miss. *I wonder if Caleb has tried to walk in a straight line in this forest recently,* she wondered to herself as she recalled his words. Trip and Marcy both nodded that they understood.

JoJo rose halfway out of her crouch and began to move away from the tree, taking cautious small steps to keep from making noise. The leaves on the forest floor were matted down and spongy, helping her attempts to move quietly. Gently pushing a couple of small branches aside, she began making her way through the underbrush, one careful step at a time. She was followed by Marcy, and then Trip, each constantly looking back expecting to see the Black Wind bursting through the bushes after them.

Crack!

JoJo froze as a look of horror covered her face. Marcy had somehow managed to step on a dead branch hidden under the wet leaves, snapping it loudly. All three kids stopped and stared at the place where the Black Wind voices had come from, holding their breath and not twitching a single muscle.

Nothing happened. JoJo slowly continued the motion she had begun, pulling a branch out of the way and moving her foot forward…

Large bodies crashed through the leafy undergrowth on both sides of the humongous oak tree, catching JoJo and her friends completely by surprise. Marcy had her sling-shot out and quickly fired off a stone, but it missed as Trip pushed her after JoJo. Three men were close behind them as JoJo quit worrying about stealth and fought her way through the annoying brush as quickly as she could, Marcy and Trip right on her heels. The men were gaining ground on them, and it would not be long before the chase was over.

JoJo came to a small clearing and instinctively decided to veer to the left, Marcy and Trip following without question. Around a few trees and she turned back hard to the right, looking ahead for something that might give them an advantage. The arrangement of impenetrable bushes, dead logs, and stout tree trunks forced her back to her left, weaving between the forest's obstacles while trying to protect her face from leafy branches that seemed intent on slapping her silly. *I don't hear anything behind us,* she thought to herself as she looked over her shoulder. *Maybe we gave them the slip back there.* As she led them into a small clearing JoJo discovered just how wrong she was.

Facing them in a short semicircle were three of the Black Wind, two of them with arrows drawn on their bows.

"Hey!" Trip complained as he crashed into Marcy and JoJo. "What's going –"

He looked up to see the cause of their sudden stop. Instantly, his hands went up defensively. "Whoa! Don't shoot, dude! You, either!" He turned slightly to include both archers.

A moment later, hands were pushing him and the girls forward as the other three Black Wind came out of the same bushes that Trip had just exited. Their ability to follow without making a sound had lulled JoJo and her friends into the belief that they nowhere close. Instead, these patrol members had played the role of 'drivers', pushing their quarry to a location like this, where the remainder of the patrol could set the trap.

"You'd best remove their weapons, no matter how primitive," commanded the tallest of the group, in the hoarse voice that the kids immediately recognized. He had been the one standing between the two bowmen, waiting for them as if he'd known this was the very spot where JoJo would lead them. "We wouldn't want any more *injuries*, would we?"

JoJo and Trip hardly noticed when the Assassins behind them took their sling-shots from their back pockets, but Marcy made a futile attempt to resist, grabbing at the wooden Y-shaped weapon as the guard removed it.

"So, I guess we now know which of these is the marksman of the group," sneered the Half-lock, raising a thin eyebrow and looking at the archer on her left. The man sported a bright red welt on the center of his forehead, and he was not smiling. "Now, lower your bows but keep your arrows nocked. If one of them tries to run, shoot him – or her – in the leg."

"What do you want with us?" JoJo asked defiantly, although she wasn't feeling quite as confident as she sounded. "Don't you guys work for the Gories?"

The Half-lock stiffened. His head was bare of any hair, a pair of short horns sticking out of each side on the top. *Just like a devil*, JoJo thought as she swallowed. His clothing appeared to be all made of smooth leather – brown pants, burgundy shirt, black boots – covered by the black cloak that symbolized the Black Wind. The Half-lock's skin had the rough look of someone who had lived a long hard life, every wrinkle and pore deeper than normal. From his right ear lobe dangled one of the hated LifeStones.

"Well, it seems that Mistress Creech was not exaggerating when she described your impertinence," he hoarsely answered. "What I require of you is your destination, Girl. You stated to our Mistress that you had urgent need to arrive quickly in Shadowrock, yet you stray from that direction and into the forest, where no one willingly goes. Why?"

The Tracker directly behind JoJo gave her a sharp shove in the back, in an effort to prompt her to answer quickly and truthfully. She hated being pushed, having been subjected to similar treatment from her older sisters ever since she could remember. She glared at the man over her shoulder before turning back to face the leader.

"We were told that this is the fastest way to Cam… Shadowrock," she lied, deciding at the very last second not to provoke the Black Wind further by saying the unspeakable name. She needed to figure a way out of this situation, not make it worse. Her brain raced as she struggled to find a solution.

"By whom?" the Half-lock demanded. "There is no one in the entire kingdom – not even the village idiots – who would claim such a thing. I think you're *lying*. And that means that you're hiding something. Something about your true purpose for detouring through these woods. What might that be?" The last question came out like a snake's hiss.

Trip and Marcy shuffled their feet nervously, neither of them wanting to join in the uncomfortable 'conversation'. For the most part, they kept their eyes on the ground, avoiding eye contact with any of their captors, especially the leader with the gruff voice. That's why they didn't see the spider land softly on JoJo's ugly black earring.

"I didn't think we needed to file a travel plan with anybody before we headed out," JoJo replied, hoping that her bravado was going to give her a little more time to think of a good answer. She knew that if she said anything about meeting the warlock that there would be trouble. Not only would Beglis run the risk of getting caught by these guys, but also JoJo and her friends would be stuck with the heavy black hoops through their ears and Caleb would not be real likely to help them anymore, no matter what he'd said about pledging his sword, et cetera.

"You would be wise not to push me, Little One. My orders are not to harm you, but I have free rein with your two friends here." He gestured with a gnarled hand that looked like it had been put through a meat-grinder and then reassembled. Badly. "Perhaps we should demonstrate. Choose one of them." It wasn't a request.

JoJo locked eyes with the Black Wind leader, refusing to look at her friends. *How do I get out of this?* She bit her lip. *I don't even know this Beglis guy, so why should I protect him over one of my best friends? But if we don't get his help, we can't save Dad. And it's not like Marcy and Trip didn't know it was going to be dangerous. Trip can take a lot more than Marcy can, so I guess I should pick him…*

It was a smallish spider, although not tiny, perhaps not quite as big as a penny when you considered it from toe to toe, or whatever they called the tips of their legs. The millions of fine hairs on its body were colored a midnight shade of blue, making it hard to detect most of the time in the dark forest. This one had descended from tree branches that were at least fifty feet above JoJo's head. The spider climbed up the LifeStone and lightly onto JoJo's ear. Her first reaction was to reach up to feel what was tickling the inside of her ear, but before she could complete the movement, she heard something that made her hand freeze in mid-air.

"I'm here to help," the spider whispered. "We're all here to help."

Chapter Sixteen

Odd Friends

JoJo turned her head from side to side, looking for whoever was whispering in her ear. She found no one near enough to be the culprit.

"Do nothing," the voice urged her. "Watch."

She wasn't the least bit sure what she was supposed to be watching for. No one else appeared to be able to hear the voice, which made her wonder if she was panicking so badly that she was starting to hear things. Her palms were beginning to feel wet...

JoJo noticed that no one was moving. Not the archers. Nor the Half-lock. They weren't even batting their eyelashes. Carefully, slowly, she turned to look over her right shoulder, spotting the Black Wind man standing behind Trip. The Tracker was completely still, almost as if frozen in place. Less cautiously, she checked the other side, and saw the same was true of the man behind Marcy. Turning all the way around, she verified that the one who had shoved her in the back was now as motionless as the others. Thankfully, the same was not true of her friends.

"What happened?" Marcy asked, staring at the men who were threatening to harm her only a minute earlier. "Why aren't they moving?"

Rather than answering, JoJo stared intently at the Black Wind patrol members, especially the leader. She noticed small movements, but it wasn't the Half-lock doing the moving. It was on his exterior. Stepping up closer, she saw.

"Thank you," she said aloud. "Now I know what was tickling my ear."

"You are welcome," the spider answered. "They are evil, these creatures that would harm you. They are no friends of the Pure."

"Hey, who are you talking to?" Trip asked, joined by Marcy in staring at their friend. "Did you say a prayer or something?"

JoJo laughed. Pointing at the Black Wind she told her two best friends, "Look closely at these guys. See the spiders crawling all over them? That's who pulled our chestnuts out of the fire."

Trip and Marcy did as she said, seeing dozens of the dark-blue arachnids moving all over each of their erstwhile captors. Slowly, a semi-translucent whitish layer was beginning to form over each of the men.

"How do you know all of this?" Marcy asked. She never liked being other than the first one to know something, especially among her peers.

"The queen spider has been sitting just inside my ear, telling me all about it," JoJo answered. Turning her head and pointing she asked, "Can you see her? Be careful!"

Marcy and Trip looked at one another before stepping uncertainly toward their friend. They jockeyed for the best position to see before Trip finally relinquished, allowing Marcy to practically stick her nose into JoJo's ear canal.

"Eek!" She immediately backed away; surprised to see exactly what she'd been told would be in there.

Trip moved in, looked quickly and softly whistled, shaking his head is near-disbelief. "I don't know if I'm more surprised that there's a spider in your ear, or that you two are having a conversation," he cracked, pulling away while still staring at the side of her head. "How long's that been going on?"

"Just started, smart-aleck," she answered. "Thank God they got here when they did."

"Are these guys dead?" Marcy asked, pointing at the men, and not sure if she should direct the question at JoJo or toward the spider. The web coverings had grown to a thickness of about an inch, slowly taking on the appearance of cocoons. JoJo waited for the spider to reply before she relayed the answer.

"No, but they're not going to bother anyone anytime soon. They're going to cover them up with enough wrapping to keep them away from us for as long as we need."

"Let me get my sling-shot before it gets lost in there," Marcy announced, wrestling her newly beloved weapon away from the grip of the webbing. Trip did the same, although with a lot less intensity. When he was done, he retrieved JoJo's as well.

While that was going on, the spider explained to JoJo that she and her friends needed to be on their way. The Half-lock was completely capable of wreaking havoc on the spiders if he was aware of their presence, and they did not want to wait around for him to return to his corrupted normal self. The effects of the nightmist spiders – as they were known – included the complete immobilization of their victims. Although the paralysis itself was not fatal, it left the recipients vulnerable to other dangers, ranging from passing predators to sudden floods. She also corrected JoJo's addressing her as the 'queen', describing herself as more of a 'Great Mother' to all of the spiders. They were of the Pure; creatures possessing natural magic rather than relying on the conjurings of witches and wizards.

The spider also told JoJo that the large boulder they were seeking was not very far from where they stood. Among the nightmist spiders, the huge rock was almost like a temple, given that underneath it is where they laid their eggs and raised their young. If the Gories and their Half-locks ever discovered that fact, they would be wiped out in one fell swoop. As such, the Great Mother was not all that pleased that Caleb had chosen the boulder as the place for them to meet the warlock. It seemed to her like an unnecessary risk, as far as the spiders were concerned.

"We promise to do our business and move away from there as quickly as possible," she stated solemnly. It felt awkward, to say the least, talking to someone she couldn't see but that she knew was sitting right there at the entrance to her ear canal. JoJo kept fighting the tendency to turn toward the voice, realizing that she would have looked like a dog chasing its tail. "Thank you again for all your help."

"Be wise in your quest, and especially your dealings with the dark ones," the spider said. "Your decisions affect more than you may know." With that, the Great Mother launched herself into the air, pulling herself back up the thread she'd used to descend.

JoJo started walking in the direction that the spider had told her, not wanting to hang around the Black Wind patrol any longer than absolutely necessary. She didn't care that they were knocked out and tied up like presents under a Christmas tree – as the Great Mother had said, it was only temporary.

"Look, they're all leaving!" Marcy announced, wonder in her voice.

JoJo and Trip turned to see what she meant, and followed her eyes upward. Hundreds of silky strands could be seen hanging from the trees above, sparkling in the filtered light like so much fine tinsel. Climbing up each shiny thread was a nightmist spider, their work done. JoJo waved, not really sure if any of them were watching, or if such a human gesture even meant anything to them. But it did to her, so she did it anyway.

"Let's go," she said finally, spinning on her heel and continuing as she had started. "As Flick keeps reminding us, there's not much time."

It didn't take them long to arrive at the giant boulder, nor was there any mistaking whether this was the correct one. The stone, probably deposited by a glacier millions of years ago, was about two stories high and at least that wide. It was smooth for the most part, with undulations and depressions that kept it from being perfectly shaped, and moss growing on parts of it.

"Holy mackerel!" Trip practically shouted when they spotted it. "That is one *big* rock."

They walked around the boulder in clockwise fashion, looking to see if the warlock was already here waiting for them. Circling the massive stone completely, they saw no one. On one side, however, JoJo did notice a wide groove in the rock that led underneath. As the groove disappeared under the boulder, she recognized a couple of the penny-sized nightmist spiders, almost as if they were standing guard.

"Maybe he's waiting up on top," JoJo thought out loud. Looking at her friends, she added, "Want to try to climb it?"

While Trip's face lit up with excitement, Marcy's headed in the other direction. Climbing was about as much fun to her as running, only worse. She had tried rock-climbing with a friend once, and it had ended painfully and full of embarrassment. She vowed that she was done with such a stupid undertaking as climbing *anything* from then on. Looking up at the imposing face of the boulder, her inner voice screamed, *Don't do it!*

"You guys go ahead. I think I'm going to stay down here, just in case this Beglis guy happens to prefer being on the ground. Like me."

JoJo smiled sympathetically at her friend, understanding that Marcy was way out of her comfort zone. Dad had taken them apple-picking in the fall, and Marcy had absolutely refused to join JoJo in climbing even the smallest of trees to shake apples down to others. Instead, she'd remained down below, happily scooping fruit off the ground and filling her bag dutifully.

Trip shrugged his shoulders and began scampering up the rock, easily finding places to grab or place his feet. Rather than finding her own way up, JoJo watched Trip and followed, using most of the same handholds. She was almost halfway up when she heard it. Trip froze, a couple of feet from the curved top.

A growl. Not a big one like a grizzly bear might make. Closer to something out of the cat family. Maybe. Another snarling noise. Whatever it was, it was close. They were starting to question the wisdom of climbing the boulder. When the beast growled again, it stuck its head over the edge of the rock, practically in Trip's face. Which turned completely white.

He lost his grip for a second, found it again, and began scrambling back down the rock face as fast as he could. There was no need to holler at JoJo – she was already well out of his way, almost to the ground. The beast followed him, snarling every step of the way.

Chapter Seventeen

Beglis

JoJo plopped to the ground in a heap, quickly gathered herself and scurried on her hands and knees to get away from the base of the boulder. She could hear the guttural growl of the animal above, and looked up to check on Trip. He decided that he was close enough to the ground to jump, pushing hard off the rock as he dropped the remaining distance. The beast – which appeared to be some cross between a raccoon, hyena, and mountain lion – prepared to leap after Trip.

Ping!

A small stone ricocheted off the granite face of the boulder. Marcy quickly readied another, mad at herself for having missed. She pulled the sling back to her ear and sighted on the creature, its small head suddenly aware of her. As Trip rolled to his feet, the second stone whizzed through the air.

And stopped. *In mid-air.* Inches before it would have struck the animal squarely in the face. The stone fell harmlessly to the ground. Marcy frowned, not sure of what she'd just seen, and pulled another smooth stone from her pouch. She was determined to make this one count.

"Halt!"

Marcy continued to draw the elastic strip back. *I'm not listening to some animal,* she thought to herself. *Of course, he's going to tell me to stop... what?* She relaxed the sling-shot slightly and stared in at the beast. It was still perched on the surface of the boulder, but no longer snarling. In fact, she could swear that the animal was holding his hands up defensively.

"Who said that?" Marcy asked, looking only at the creature. The voice didn't belong to either of her companions, and she wasn't going to take her eyes off the animal anyways. Trip and JoJo had taken up positions behind her, especially after they saw that she was firing away with her deadly sling-shot.

"It wasn't us," JoJo offered, still breathing hard, but not as hard as Trip was. Pointing a shaky finger at the beast, she said, "I think it was him."

"Of course it was me," the animal replied in a voice as refined as a Harvard professor's. "Who else were you shooting at?"

"Well, you shouldn't have been chasing my friends," Marcy responded, defending herself. Trip arched an eyebrow at the reference to him as one of her friends, but kept his mouth shut, figuring the time wasn't right to question her choice of words. "What are you, anyway?"

It figures, JoJo thought silently. *Faced with a man-eating beast, and Marcy the academic wants to know what kind of animal it is. Sheesh.* She looked at her friend incredulously.

Before any of the kids could say another word, the creature began to change right in front of their eyes. The facial features softened in such a way that it actually started taking on the appearance of a human, although difficult to tell whether male or female. At the same time, the body was lengthening while fur turned enchantingly into clothes. Magic. Clinging to the side of the huge boulder was a man in a dark brown pin-striped suit.

"What I *was*," he said, leaping gracefully to the ground and landing softly on his feet, "is known commonly as a Glutton, a savage beast that backs down from virtually nothing, no matter what the size difference might be. In some places, it is called a wolverine. Either way, it's a useful shape for me to assume when I'm out and about. What I am now, however, is your ally."

"Let me guess," JoJo said, stepping forward. "You're Beglis, aren't you?"

The man bowed elegantly. "At your service," he added. "I thought you'd be here earlier, and then I heard there was some trouble nearby, so I decided not to take any chances. Especially not with a Half-lock roaming the forest."

Now that he was standing on level ground and in human form, the warlock was not so intimidating. In fact, he looked more like a local banker than some sinister wizard or half-cocked magician. Streaks of silver lined his temples, highlighting dark brown hair that covered all but the top of his head. There was nothing handsome or ugly about the man, merely normal. Under any other circumstances, his face would probably have been forgotten five minutes after the kids walked away. These were hardly 'other circumstances', however.

"Oh, man!" Trip exclaimed. "If you're the guy who can get these honking earrings off of us, you'll be my new best friend. I swear it!" He grabbed his LifeStone as if Beglis might not know what he was talking about.

"Ah, yes. The Free Knight mentioned that you would be seeking my assistance along those lines." Beglis rubbed his chin as if he might be thinking about how to deal with the problem. "I think that we might be able to reach some mutually acceptable accommodation."

"What do you mean?" JoJo asked suspiciously. "Are you talking about making some kind of *deal*? I thought Caleb said you're on our side."

"I am on no one's *side*, dear girl, except my own," the warlock answered smoothly. "I have not survived the past ten centuries by catering to the whims of every passing crusader, intent on overthrowing the evil powers-that-be. Not at all. There is great risk in tampering with the dark magicks put into place by Grimm and his witch-spawn, and I do not confront that risk without compensation. No, if you would like my help then I suggest *very strongly* that you come to the table willing to strike a bargain. Otherwise, I think that our business here is done, and I shall return to my more mundane daily routine."

"Are you blackmailing us?" Marcy demanded, eyes wide. She still held the sling-shot in front of her, relaxed and at waist-level, with one hand on the wooden handle and the other clutching the stone. Her body tensed as she grew excited. "Seriously?"

Beglis sniffed and looked at her as if she had greatly offended him. "Blackmail? That is a serious charge indeed. I should think 'barter' is a better description of what I've put forth to you. We are merely trading my services for whatever you have to offer. Of equal value, of course."

"Of course," JoJo parroted. She motioned with one hand for Marcy to relax, the sling-shot having come up a bit in the past few seconds. "What exactly do you think we have that we could offer you? I mean, we don't even have any money, or anything else valuable."

"Ah, that's the spirit!" Beglis smiled as he rubbed his hands together. "My sources tell me that you may actually know the location of the *Chrimeus*…" He let that hang in the air so that he could gauge their reactions.

Trip and Marcy both started to say something, but stopped when JoJo held up her hands. She bit her lip and stared at the thousand-year old warlock, trying to determine if he was attempting to cheat them out of something.

"What if we do?" she asked, sticking her chin out like she was back on the playground in elementary school.

"Well, I believe that I would consider a trade, as it were," he answered, smiling and holding his hands together in front of his chest. "I will remove those dastardly shackles from your ear lobes in exchange for the *Chrimeus*, should you actually locate and acquire it. And survive long enough to get it back here to me."

JoJo continued to bite her lip, so much so that she threatened to draw her own blood shortly. She thought about what the warlock was asking, and shook her head. The Gories had already demanded the *Chrimeus* as the price for releasing her father, so she doubted that she'd be able to satisfy both the witches and Beglis. At the same time, all she had to do right now was to *promise* him that he'd be the one to get it, if and when they found the darned thing. When the time actually came, she could still do whatever it took to save Dad. Once these stinking earrings were off, she didn't plan on passing through this neck of the woods ever again.

Marcy and Trip stared at her, trying to understand what was going through her head. They both knew that the decision was hers to make because it was her father.

"Don't do it," Marcy advised in a half-whisper. "We'll figure out another way to get rid of the LifeStones."

"She's right," Trip added surprisingly. Reaching up to his LifeStone, he continued, "I hate these things as much as anyone, but if we don't give that special whatchamacallit to the witches… I mean, that was the whole reason we came here, right? To save your dad; not run errands for this guy." He jerked his thumb toward Beglis, who was watching and waiting patiently.

JoJo turned from her friends and faced the well-dressed warlock. She forced herself to quit biting her lip. Visions of her Dad in a dark dungeon danced through her head. So did pictures of little children being snatched from villages around the country. The Gories plucked at the children, removing their souls and replacing them with some evil essence, causing horns to grow on their heads like the Half-lock they'd seen earlier. JoJo shook her head to get rid of the images.

"We'll do it," she said, looking Beglis in the eyes. "As soon as we get my Dad free, we'll bring the *Chrimeus* here to you. Right to this very spot."

"Excellent. Then we have a deal." He clapped his hands sharply twice, and the air shook as if a shock wave had passed through.

Lying at their feet were the broken pieces of their LifeStones. All three kids reached up to verify that their ears were once again naked, free of the hideous jewels. Relief swept through each of them, the idea that they were no longer tagged by the Gories.

When they looked up to thank the warlock, he was gone. Whether he left as man or Glutton, they had no idea.

Chapter Eighteen

Are We There Yet?

It was starting to get dark by the time they left the forest, although it was lighter than it had been in the woods. Based on what the Half-lock had said about the forest road taking them out of the way, JoJo convinced the others that they should go back out to the main trail heading away from the village. Navigating their way from the boulder back to the forest road hadn't been all that difficult, especially when compared to looking for the giant rock. It helped that they didn't have half a dozen men chasing them.

Their legs were sore and heavy from all the walking and running. Amazingly, no one had blisters yet. Not so surprising was the fact that Marcy's wasn't the only stomach grumbling now. They hadn't eaten anything since the dried biscuits and shrunken apples that Caleb had provided earlier, and that had seemed like days ago. Not to mention, it wasn't like it had been a real meal like pancakes and sausage or something. What any of them would give for a pepperoni pizza right about now…

"How are we going to find this place?" Trip asked, trying not to think about how hungry he was becoming. "The last time we asked for help didn't go too smoothly, you know what I mean?"

"Yeah, I know," JoJo answered, somewhat annoyed. "I was there, too. We should've asked that Beglis character."

"Well, he didn't give us much chance," Marcy chipped in. She had been surprisingly quiet during their trek out of the forest, apparently too miserable to even complain. "If we'd have known he was going to disappear like that, we could've made sure we got all our questions in before accepting his… bargain."

She said the last word hesitantly, still not sure if she agreed with the deal JoJo had struck with the warlock. Something told her that you don't go around intentionally reneging on contracts with magical beings, especially ones that chose to make themselves into wolverines whenever they wanted to go for a stroll. She didn't know how her friend planned to *not* turn the *Chrimeus* over to the Gories, if they even managed to find the darned thing in the first place. Also, something about Caleb that didn't add up quite right kept gnawing at the back of her mind.

"Hey guys, why would Caleb help us find the *Chrimeus* if he knows we plan to hand it to the Pewtris Grimm and his daughters?" She looked across at JoJo and Trip, trying to gauge their reactions in the dusky twilight. "After what he said, it seems like there's no way on earth that he'd want that to end up in the Lord of Evil's dirty paws."

"Well, he's my Dad's friend and fellow Free Knight, if *that* whole thing is true," JoJo answered, but without much conviction in her voice. She still had a hard time wrapping her head around the notion that her father led a completely different life in another world, even if it had been before coming to Ferry Village. *Why wouldn't he have told any of us? I wonder if Mom knew about any of this.* "So maybe he just wants to help us rescue Dad, and then deal with the *Chrimeus* afterward."

Marcy gave her a look that said how lame she thought JoJo's answer was. She was too tired, too sore, and way too hungry to argue, so she let it go. They walked in silence until nightfall completely set in. Happily, there were no sounds other than their own footsteps, save for an occasional owl hooting in the distance.

Just when Marcy was convinced that she could go no further, they saw a light directly ahead of them. At first, it looked as if it were coming from a solitary source, like a single candle or torch. As they moved toward it, they realized that it was the glow from an entire village or town.

"Do you think that's Camelot?" Trip asked, too tired to remember which name to use for their destination.

"I dunno," JoJo answered, squinting into the night like her friends. "Kind of hard to tell from here. Sure would help if these people put up a sign or two on the road every once in a while."

"I don't care, as long as there's a place where we can get off our feet and get something to eat," Marcy moaned predictably.

"Hopefully, these people are friendlier than everyone else we've met in this place," Trip said, echoing what the others were thinking. "We haven't exactly had a lot of luck with anyone besides Caleb."

They picked up their pace noticeably, the thought of hot food and a place to sit down driving them with renewed energy. Even Marcy was able to draw upon physical reserves that she didn't know she had, focusing her attention on the growing light instead of the gnawing pangs in her tummy. It seemed to take forever to close the distance, but eventually the single light resolved itself into several, then many lights. By the time they arrived at the tall gated wall, another hour had passed.

JoJo craned her neck to look up at the top of the wall, directly above the gate. This structure was a great deal sturdier than what they had seen at the village, with its primitive wooden timbers fastened together. The wall in front of them was constructed of stone blocks, like she would have imagined the outside of a castle to look like. She'd never seen a real castle, of course, so her only references were what she'd seen on television or at the movies.

The main gate – a pair of massive wooden doors reinforced with wide bands of black iron – were closed, *probably for the night*, JoJo thought to herself. She spied what she considered a normal-sized door to the right, although it looked tiny compared to the massive gate. It was also closed, but she figured that it was their way in. Trip caught her arm just as she started in that direction.

"You know, we're not wearing those goofy earrings, so someone's going to pitch a fit as soon as we walk through that door."

As if to confirm what he was saying, they all reached up and felt their right earlobes. Thankfully, they were bare. Unfortunately, they might as well have neon signs over their heads. Before they could discuss it any further, they heard a ruckus on the other side of the door. Voices, mostly men but also one loud woman.

"Who's down there?" a male voice shouted down from high up on the wall. JoJo, Marcy and Trip tipped their heads way back to look up at the man. His face was in shadows, backlit by torches behind him. Luckily, there were no such lights on the outside of the wall, helping to obscure the details of their appearance. Such as whether they were wearing LifeStones.

"Just us kids from Fer-... from the village," JoJo answered. "We're looking –"

The small door burst open just then, cutting her off. A short, slightly heavy woman bustled out, flapping her hands and talking up a storm at the same time. She was joined by a guard whose armor partially reflected the light from inside the walls, and who was carrying his own torch as well.

"I *told* you they were out here," she fussed at the guard, who appeared to be trying both to accompany her and avoid her busy hands at the same time. She turned to face him, pushing him in the center of his breastplate. "Why don't you wait right here? These children aren't used to seeing real soldiers and I don't want them frightened to the point of running off into the night. I've been waiting half the day for them as it is." Taking a step back, she checked to make sure the guard was going to do as she suggested before turning back to the children.

She held her arms out wide as she approached JoJo and her friends. They could see that she was older, like a grandmother with silvery hair glowing in the torchlight. Of course, that hair was pulled back and tied off, revealing the large, odious LifeStone dangling from her small ear.

"Call me 'Maude'", she whispered as she reached them. "And put these fake LifeStones on your ears." She hugged JoJo, leaving her hands open so that the others could pluck the black hoops from them, then pulling her arms back enough for JoJo to get hers. As sneakily as they could, they managed to attach the new earrings without the guards figuring it out.

"What took you three so long?" Maude asked loud enough for the guards to hear. "I've been worried sick the past few hours."

"We're sorry," JoJo answered, also a little extra loudly, understanding the game but still unsure of who this little old woman was. "We got sidetracked a little bit."

Maude tugged at all three of them gently, herding them toward the door and the waiting guard. "Well, let's get you inside, nice and proper. You must be famished."

Under her breath, Marcy answered, "You have no idea."

The guard eyed them suspiciously as they all passed in front of him on their way through the door. Not only was it unusual for children to be outside of the gates without an adult escort, it was even stranger at night. And these kids seemed bizarre in other ways as well – their hair was not tied back in the fashion dictated by the realm, and their clothing was extremely different. Maude placed herself between her guests and the soldier, proceeded through the door and then hustled them quickly away from the gate. At this hour, there were not many people about, save those on guard duty.

They found themselves inside a large fortified town, many times larger than the village they'd encountered earlier that day. Buildings rose up several stories high on either side of the cobblestoned main street, which Maude quickly had them exit, turning down a dirt alley to the right. When it was apparent that no one was listening, JoJo stopped. The others followed suit, all with questions on their faces.

"All right, lady," she whispered urgently, "we really appreciate your helping us through the gate and all, and that food you were talking about sounds pretty darned good, but who *are* you?"

"I told you already," she answered with a kind smile, wrinkles at the corners of her eyes. "I'm Maude. Caleb told me to take care of you."

Chapter Nineteen

Maude

"So, tell us how you know Caleb," Marcy said between bites. Maude had prepared a modest meal for them: a meaty stew with onions, carrots and cabbage mixed in, along with a couple loaves of warm, crusty bread. Marcy didn't normally eat a lot of meat, but she was so hungry that she wasn't about to be picky. What she didn't want to know was the *type* of animal that the meat came from. For all she knew, she was enjoying the best porcupine stew she'd ever tasted.

Her companions had no such qualms about their dietary habits. While both JoJo's Dad and Trip's mom were decent enough cooks, it was uncommon for them to have the luxury of the time needed to prepare meals from scratch. As a result, the majority of dining in both the Mallory and Dowling households came out of boxes and cans. A grilled-cheese sandwich was considered fine cuisine on most days. Trip was already finishing his second bowl of the stew, and had polished off one of the bread loaves by himself.

"Oh, Caleb and I go back many, many years," Maude answered, moving around the table to refill their cups with sweet ale. She sat the pitcher in the middle of the heavy wooden table before settling herself into a chair at one end. Surprising her guests, she reached into the folds of her dress and pulled out a pipe. From some other hidden recess of her clothing she withdrew a small leather pouch with a drawstring pulled tight. Not paying any attention to the three middle-schoolers for the time being, she went through a very deliberate process of loading tobacco from the pouch into the bowl of the pipe, and then returning the leather bag to its usual location deep within the vest that she wore over her dress. She reached for a long, slender piece of wood that resembled a chopstick – although somewhat longer – and held one end over the table candle closest to her. Once it caught, she held the fire over the tobacco-stuffed bowl and drew steadily, sucking the flame down into the aromatic dried leaves. When she was satisfied, she blew on the burning stick and set it back on the table, now half its original length and smoldering a bit at one end. Maude puffed mightily on the pipe several more times, then exhaled a cloud of smoke and sat back comfortably.

Marcy coughed once, more out of reflex than anything else. No one in her household had ever smoked anything, and she had never even sat around a campfire before, so she was bracing for what she believed would be an unpleasant onslaught against her sense of smell. Trip had been around plenty of older men who smoked a variety of cigars, cigarettes, and even pipes. In fact, he had come to think of this as normal, despite the general movement of society toward the other direction. JoJo, on the other hand, was completely transfixed. Not by what she had just seen of the old woman's ritual, but rather by the rich, pungent aroma. She recognized that smell.

"Let's see, where to start?" Maude mused aloud as she blew occasional smoke rings toward the high ceiling. "I guess you children already know about the Free Knights, so I don't need to bore you with that history lesson. Except to say that the Knights do not act alone. That's where I come in, and people like me. We're known simply as Friends these days, but originally the full title was Friends and Supporters of the Free Knights of Camelot."

Marcy choked on her stew, her eyes opening wide. "Aren't you worried about *saying* that?" she managed to sputter.

Maude chuckled. "Oh, I see that you've heard about the 'unspeakable' name. That mostly applies if you're wearing one of those despicable stones on your ears. These imitation LifeStones, such as we have on, are to avoid unwanted harassment. Pewtris Grimm and his witch-daughters do not exert control over us, cannot track our whereabouts, and do not care what words we mutter." Before her guests could argue with the last part, she added, "Well, usually, that is."

"But why doesn't everybody do that?" JoJo asked, feeling the counterfeit LifeStone still hanging from her right ear. It wasn't anywhere near as heavy as the real one was, and it didn't seem to bother her as much, probably because it exerted no real power over her. "I mean, assuming they could find a warlock or someone like that to remove their LifeStones."

"That's just it, child. Most people don't really want to be separated from the dastardly ear hoops. Over the centuries since they were first introduced, these wool-headed fools have come to believe that the LifeStones actually protect them from evil rather than allow evil to control them."

"So, they bought the story hook, line and sinker?" Trip asked, a look of doubt across his face. "Not a single person said 'no'?"

"Oh there were a few in the beginning," Maude answered, "but after the Gories made those rebellious souls explode into millions of pieces or turn into snakes or some other horrible retribution, that put an end to the resistance."

"Except for you." JoJo was half-smiling at the old woman. "What's your story?"

"It's not just me," Maude replied, pouring a cup of the sweet ale for herself. She gestured for her guests to help themselves if they wanted any more. "As I said, I'm a Friend. There are more of us than there are Free Knights, but that's not to say that we number a great many. In this town, I am one of three Friends, although I don't know the identities of the other two and they do not know mine. At least, I hope they don't. It prevents the Black Wind from being able to torture information that would have us all rounded up at once, should they ever discover one of us as a Friend. We learned our lessons late." She said this last sentence with deep sadness.

"What happened?" Marcy asked, finally unable to put another bite in her mouth. She pushed the empty bowl to the center of the table and sat back, her stomach completely full. Her curiosity was as much intellectual as anything else.

Maude had let her pipe go out and made no attempt to relight it. Instead she stuck it in her mouth from time to time, as if it helped her gather her thoughts. She went on to tell the sixth-graders about the rise and fall of the Free Knights. It was history, but not like any history class any of them had ever sat through before. The kindly old woman's eyes sparkled as she spoke of the majesty of the Knights, even though their existence was supposed to be kept secret from Pewtris Grimm until the time was right for taking their kingdom back.

That never happened, and now twelve Knights remained out of almost five hundred. Twelve.

The Knights knew that they couldn't overthrow Grimm without strengthening their numbers considerably, and that that was going to take time. They were also well aware of the need for reliable supporters who could provide aid in many forms. The Friends and Supporters of the Free Knights of Camelot were sworn to secrecy and loyalty under penalty of death. In attempting to ensure even greater fidelity, the Friends were chosen only from the bloodlines of Knights

"So, like your father or grandfather was a Free Knight, Maude?" JoJo asked when she finished her tale. The familiar aroma of the tobacco tugged at her.

"Actually, it's my son," Maude answered, pushing a wisp of hair out of her face. "And as far as I know, he still *is* a Free Knight, although I haven't seen him in many years."

"Oh, he's one of the twelve?" Marcy asked, perking up. "That's great that he survived."

"That's cool," Trip added, looking at JoJo for a reaction. It wasn't what he expected.

She was crying. "Where's your son now, Maude?" she managed through whimpers, but she already knew the answer.

"Caleb seems to think he may be a prisoner. The one in Camelot."

Chapter Twenty

On the Move Again

JoJo tried to fight off whoever was attempting to wake her up. Despite how tired she'd been, sleep had not come easily as she digested so many changes to what she thought she'd known about her life. It had all hit her like an avalanche. While her two best friends had fallen immediately to sleep on the straw beds Maude had arranged on the floor for them, JoJo tossed and turned, trying to process all of this new information about the man she had thought she knew so well. The whole Free Knight thing had been quite a load by itself, but now she had a *grandmother*, too? She could swear that she'd just dozed off minutes earlier…

"Come now, sleepy-head," the voice urged her, somehow related to the hands that were shaking her gently. "We need to get you three out of the town before sunrise. I set some clothes out for you that won't look quite so queer."

Marcy and Trip were already sitting at the big wooden table, helping themselves to hot biscuits topped with honey. Mugs of steaming tea sat in front of each of them. JoJo wiped the stubborn sleep from her eyes and stumbled to one of the benches. Through the single window in the room she could see that it was still dark outside, but it was light enough inside the kitchen to notice the new outfits her friends were wearing. Like the ensemble that Maude had laid out for her, the clothing that Marcy and Trip now wore looked like something straight out of Hansel and Gretel, but a lot more drab and dull.

"You have a great deal of ground to cover, especially on foot," Maude said, smiling softly at her young house-guests. "Also, it's probably best that we not allow the gate guards to have too good a look at you, no matter how much we dress you in 'normal' clothing."

This last statement caused Marcy and Trip to look down and check out their outfits. Marcy wore a shirt and vest over a long skirt, all in the latest grays and browns. She didn't worry too much about how the skirt would hinder her running because everything hindered her running, especially her flabby out-of-shape legs. Trip considered the rough trousers and off-white cotton shirt that replaced his dark jeans and hockey shirt, and shrugged his shoulders. He could have done without the hat, but Maude had explained that he stuck out more with his short hair than anything else. As long as he could reclaim his stuff and ditch the hat before he showed his face in Ferry Village again, he was okay. They both shook the old woman's comment off and continued their breakfast.

JoJo couldn't help staring at Maude. *After all this time, I really do have a grandmother!* she thought to herself as she helped herself to a flaky biscuit. Good God, what's next – am I going to find out that I've got a brother, too? She drizzled some of the thick, gooey honey over the biscuit before breaking off a piece and sticking it in her month. Her stomach still felt full after the meal of the previous night, which seemed like it was just a little while ago. Nevertheless, they all knew that it could be a while before they got another chance to stuff their faces with something this good.

"What's the plan?" she asked, sipping hot tea from the nearest mug. She had given up her worn, faded jeans and sweater for a boyish pair of pants and shirt, much like what Trip was wearing. At her age, she could easily pass for a boy.

Maude looked at her very differently than she had the night before. The older woman practically beamed at her granddaughter, wanting to drink in every moment with her new-found blood relative. The smile on her lips was exceeded by the one in her eyes.

"First, we will make our way to the East Gate, opposite from the one through which you entered the town yesterday. That will put you on the old King's Road leading to Camelot. That road shortly joins the Crystalline River, running alongside its southern bank all the way to the city. I will accompany you part-way to the river, long enough to put some distance between you and the town guards. Unfortunately, I have speed to match my age, and would only be a drag on your need for haste, so I will part company with you much sooner than I would wish." She sniffed a little as she finished. The three kids looked into their mugs to avoid her eyes.

The East Gate was barely visible behind them as the first light of day began to peek over the horizon, casting a pinkish glow across the sky. Thanks to Maude's brusque quick-talking, they hadn't had any problems with the gate guard. It helped that he was probably very tired from a long night of staring into the dark nothingness outside the town walls, and was ready for someone else to relieve him so he could go home and sleep. The last thing he wanted was to get tied up with some cranky old woman taking her grandchildren out to visit relatives in Dimwell or wherever she said. Maude was counting on the assumption that the guard's replacement would have no questions as to why she was returning to the town alone.

"Please tell me about your sisters," Maude said as she walked alongside JoJo. Marcy and Trip trailed slightly behind, not wanting to interrupt the time their best friend had with her grandmother, now that she found out she had one still living. Even if it was in another world.

On many occasions, JoJo had confided to Marcy that she'd really envied kids who had grandparents to go hang out with and get spoiled by. Obviously, she missed having a mother, but this was different. Marcy understood, and tried not to go into too much detail whenever her own grandparents bought her nice things or took her out to eat at nice restaurants. JoJo's mother's parents had never been available to visit, always claiming bad health or some conflict that was apparently more important than seeing their daughter and grandchildren. They lived far enough away that it was too much of a financial strain for JoJo and her family to fly out to see them. In the end, they'd passed away several years ago, not long after Mrs. Mallory had jumped off the bridge.

JoJo painted a much nicer picture of her sisters to Maude than she ever did to Trip and Marcy. She described Maggie as the caring, oldest sister who had been suddenly burdened with the responsibility of helping to raise three siblings when their mother died unexpectedly. Between school, housework, a job as a waitress at Uncle Andy's coffee shop, and helping her younger sisters, Maggie still managed to find time for a boyfriend. Although only a year younger, Ronnie was a great deal less responsible and much more worldly than Maggie, spending as little time in Ferry Village as she could get away with, while wrapping half the boys in town around her little finger. Her great goal in life was to get out of

Maine and move to someplace warm and sunny, like California or

Florida, as soon as possible. Of course, Maude had no idea of what

JoJo was referring to, but smiled nonetheless. Last, there was Scrap,

whose real name was Anabel. She was an eight-year old ball of fire,

forever getting into fights at school, usually with boys older and

bigger than her. Scrap was a good athlete, too, especially when it

came to baseball. She'd made every all-star team possible, ever

since she started playing as a four-year old.

"I should very much like to meet them," Maude said

wistfully when JoJo finished. She stopped in the middle of the road,

the others forced to do likewise. "Whether that means that I must

travel to your world or they come here, whatever it takes. You will

tell them about me, won't you?"

"Of course I will!" JoJo blurted. "I mean, they're not going

to *believe* me at first, but they're probably not going to believe most

of what I tell them about all of this." She made a sweeping motion

with her hand, as if to take in everything that had happened since

Flick showed up in her bedroom.

"Well then, this is where I must leave you," the old woman announced, her eyes watering. She spread her arms wide and wrapped them lovingly around JoJo, mumbling for her granddaughter to take care and come back safely while patting her on the back several times. Releasing her, she took a step back and then proceeded to hug Marcy and Trip in turn, although not as long or vigorously as she had JoJo. Composing herself, she said, "Now I want you to stay on this road down to the river. When you get there, try to buy passage on a boat. It's much faster than walking, and you haven't much time. Here's enough money for the three of you."

She handed a small pouch that contained heavy coins to JoJo, who stuck it in the front pocket of the baggy pants Maude had given her. She had to tighten her rope-belt to fight against the weight of the coins, but she wanted to keep her hands free as much as possible. Even though they had Marcy with them, there was no telling when she or Trip might need to use their sling-shots, also. Or worse.

Before the departure could get any more uncomfortable, Maude turned and headed back toward the town, her head bent slightly downward but her stride steady. JoJo couldn't see her crying, but she noticed the occasional shudder of the old woman's shoulders as she walked away, and she guessed as much. Wiping the corners of her own eyes, she spun around and headed toward the river, forcing her two best friends in the world to follow and catch up.

"How awesome is that?" she said, looking straight ahead and surprising both Trip and Marcy. "I've got a grandmother and she's about as cool as they get."

No one answered because it wasn't really a question. Marcy was happy for her. Trip figured that he got a grandmother out of this, too, even if not exactly by blood. Over his shoulder hung a bag loaded with bread, fruit, and dried meats. *That's what grandmas are for*, he thought happily to himself.

It only took them less than an hour to reach the edge of the Crystalline River. The water seemed to run lazily at this point, and the far bank was at least half a football field away. There wasn't any bridge that they could see, but they spotted a flat ferry boat that operated right there in front of them. The road they'd been on ended in a T-intersection with one that ran along the river – the King's Road. Even at this early hour there were travelers in wagons, on foot, and on horseback scattered up and down the King's Road.

Of special interest to JoJo and her friends was a group of six black-cloaked horsemen coming up from the direction that they wanted to go. Black Wind. Again.

"Down to the river," JoJo said urgently. "Quick, but don't run!"

The only boat on the riverfront was the flat-bottomed ferry, and it was getting ready to push off to make its journey to the other side of the river. Whatever boat Maude had in mind for them to purchase a ride on hadn't shown up yet, or maybe didn't even exist. The mounted patrol had picked up speed, as if they had recognized the young troublemakers. They would be there in no time.

"Jump on the boat!" JoJo yelled to Trip and Marcy. "Now!"

The boat was already three feet from the embankment and moving away with the assistance of a man pushing a long pole into the water. JoJo made the leap easily, as did Trip, both landing on their feet while startling the ferryman. Marcy stood staring at them from the shore. Paralyzed.

The Black Wind horses kicked up dust behind her as they pulled to a stop.

"C'mon, Marcy! Jump, for crying out loud!" JoJo shouted as the boat continued to pull away. Six feet. Eight feet. The first Black Wind rider dismounted. Ten feet.

Marcy backed up a couple of steps, looking for all the world like she was going to just give up and surrender herself to the approaching black-cloaked... And then she took off.

Chapter Twenty-one

Waterborne

No one at Mahoney Middle School would have believed it, not in a million years. Marcella 'the Marshmallow' DiPietro had somehow drawn upon her inner-athlete self and bolted like a track star. Reaching the very edge of the river bank, she exploded into a long jump for the ages. Her form had been less than graceful, including how her mouth was shaped weirdly as she shouted, but the result was stupendous. Somehow, Marcy had sailed over twelve feet through the air, skirt flapping, and barely landed on the very end of the flatboat. JoJo and Trip each grabbed an arm to keep her from falling backward into the water.

"Oh my God, Marcy," JoJo stammered. "That was incredible!"

"Dude, that was awesome!" Trip added. Marcy wasn't sure if she was more amazed by her own physical act or by the compliments she was getting from the school's biggest Jock. She sat on the wooden floor of the ferry, catching her breath.

"Uh oh," JoJo muttered. "This can't be good." Trip and Marcy followed her eyes.

The dismounted Black Wind rider was signaling for the ferryman to reverse course and return to shore. From the calm way that he was silently giving the order, it didn't appear that he was used to being disobeyed. They felt the boat slow.

The three middle-schoolers weren't the only ones trying to cross the river on this particular ferry. Besides the ferryman, there was a farmer with a pair of oxen, and a family with all of their meager belongings. None of them looked happy to have to return to the riverbank, anxious for their own reasons to be on the other side.

"Mister, don't do it!" Trip urged, standing up and facing the ferryman.

The boat operator wore no shoes, and his pant-legs ended above his calves. His sleeveless shirt was open at the collar, revealing a white-haired chest. Every muscle on this man's body had been worked a thousand times a day for every day that he could remember. Poling this craft against the pull of the river several times a day had been his life since he was a boy. It hadn't been an easy life, but it could be worse. A lot worse. Like, for instance, if he disobeyed the dark-cloaked witch's pet directing him from the shore right now. That wasn't going to happen. Not today. Not for some snot-nosed boat-jumpers trying to hitch a free ride.

"Yer lucky I don't gut ya with me fishin' knife, boy. Yer two girlies as well. I don't take to free-loaders, and I damn well don't take to anyone that gets me inta trouble with the black bloggers there." Unsmiling, he waved acknowledgment to the Tracker on shore, and moved to the other end of the boat so that he could push in the other direction.

"What're we going to do?" Marcy asked, suddenly deflated that her miraculous jump had been for nothing. She looked at the water with despair. "And before you even consider it, I can't swim well enough to make it across this river. Even without the current. Even if I had a swimsuit on instead of this get-up."

JoJo bit her lip nervously. She looked from the ferryman, now poling from the other end of the boat, to the shore, where the other Black Wind were still up on their horses. Two of the black-cloaked men had arrows strung on their bows. JoJo knew that they were safe from being seriously hurt by the Black Wind because of her bargain with Creech the Gorie. But that wouldn't necessarily stop these guys from shooting someone else on the boat

"We don't have time for this," she muttered annoyingly. "Trip, do you think you could push that boat guy into the water? You know, so we can take this thing over?"

"Seriously?" He said a little too loudly. "That dude's twice my size and as hard as a rock. He'll probably grab me by the back of the neck and snap me in half or something. Besides, then what would we do? I doubt we could get this thing across the river without the guy."

JoJo looked at the riverbank that they'd just left. It was getting nearer as they sat there, the ferryman having reversed the direction of the boat. In another minute or two, they'd be close enough for the Black Wind man to jump down next to them. She stood up.

"Let's go," she said, heading toward the other end. Trip and Marcy did as she said, both keeping a watchful eye on the Tracker looming closer. All three of them picked up speed just as the black-cloaked man landed on the boat where they'd been crouching a minute earlier. The boat bumped roughly against the embankment, nearly knocking JoJo and her friends off their feet.

They recovered their balance and made their way around the huge oxen, who didn't seem the least bit bothered by all the back-and-forth change of direction and bumping of the boat. The Tracker followed after them, unfazed by animals or passengers or pretty much anything, as well. Near the end of the deck sat a medium-sized barrel that JoJo hoped wasn't too full. When she got to it, she turned to her friends.

"Trip, help me push this in the water. Marcy, sling-shot that guy, will you?" Whispering to Trip, she continued, "As soon as she takes that Black Wind dude out, we need to get her in the water. This barrel's going to be her floatey, like they use for little kids."

He made a face, wincing. "She isn't going to like it."

JoJo shrugged.

Marcy already had her stone on the way by the time the Tracker realized what was going on. Too late. He crumpled to the deck like a sack of potatoes as the projectile ricocheted off of his forehead. Commotion sounded immediately from the Half-lock leading this patrol of the Black Wind. The barrel splashed into the water. Marcy felt hands grabbing her while she still watched for the trouble behind them. Without warning, she was pulled off the end of the flatboat by her two companions.

They hit the water and began thrashing right away. Trip and JoJo had swum fully clothed on more than one occasion, usually in the frozen waters of Casco Bay when they'd fallen off the ice flows near the shores of Ferry Village. They had never had to actually swim very far in those circumstances, although they had had the extra burden of winter coats over their other clothing. Marcy, on the other hand, had never experienced anything remotely similar to what they were now doing. Or trying to do.

"Get the barrel!" she heard JoJo shout, obviously to Trip since there was no way that *she* was going to get anything. Marcy coughed up some water as she struggled to kick her legs, helplessly tangled in the long skirt. She could see JoJo just ahead of her, but no sign of Trip. Water splashed in her eyes, making it even more difficult to make any progress. Panic started to set in as she felt herself drifting with the current. JoJo was no longer in sight.

Oh my God. Is this how it all ends? I haven't even kissed a boy yet! Not counting my cousin Ralph, of course, which was gross. What's going to happen to Lucky? I mean, I know my family will feed him and let him outside, but will anyone play with him anymore? What about my science project? I wish I... The water was all around her as Marcy rolled along like a piece of driftwood, no longer splashing with the effort to stay afloat. Light played funny games with her vision, as the rays of sun refracted through the moving water, creating all sorts of bizarre patterns. She even thought she saw a giant tortoise...

Marcy tried to cough the water out of her lungs as her head rose above the river surface. Just her head. And she was moving. That's when she realized that she was sitting on something solid. She reached up and pulled the wet hair out of her face, wiping her eyes. *What the...?* She looked all around as the water whipped past both sides of her neck. On her right, horsemen in black cloaks were riding hard to keep pace with her. On her left, she only saw the wide expanse of the river, with the far bank occasionally spotted with trees and shrubs. *Where are JoJo and Trip?*

She tried to look down through the water to determine what she was sitting on, but it was difficult because of the sunlight reflecting in every which direction and the fact that her face was too close to the surface to allow her to see clearly. *How in the world am I not falling off this thing, whatever it is?*

"Hey Marcy, what do you think of our rides?" She heard JoJo's voice over the choppy river water and tried to locate her. After what seemed like an eternity, she finally found her very dear friend cruising along behind and to her left. At first, she had thought it was just a chunk of wood bobbing along down the river. Trying to ignore the Black Wind on the other side of her, she strained to rise

up and peer over the waves to get a better look.

"Where's Trip?" she asked, probably a little too anxiously.

She was just concerned for his well-being, she told herself. "And

what the heck are we riding on?"

"He's right behind me," JoJo hollered back, spitting water as

she spoke. "He's mad about losing all the food that Maude had

given us. And our transportation is being provided by a few of

Flick's friends. They're called Fast Turtles."

Fast Turtles? You're kidding me, right? That explains the

giant tortoise... "You know that there's no such thing as Fast

Turtles, don't you? That's what you call an oxymoron." Marcy

shouted back over her shoulder.

"The only morons I see are the ones trying to keep up with us

on horseback," JoJo laughed.

Marcy returned her attention to the riverbank on her right.

Sure enough, the flapping black cloaks were steadily losing ground, drifting further and further behind. *I can't believe we don't have any food!*

Chapter Twenty-two

Another Detour

"Where'd they come from and why are they helping us?" Marcy asked, no longer having to shout to be heard. The three Fast Turtles were now traveling alongside one another, although they maintained the same speed as before. They had also risen a little bit, so that now their riders sat with their chests out of the water.

JoJo explained that when they'd jumped off the ferry boat, the plan had been to swim to the far side of the river and that the barrel was intended to give Marcy something to hold onto. When the barrel got away, Trip tried to swim after it but got swept up in the stronger current of the river's center. JoJo then attempted to help him, and lost Marcy in the process. For a very scary few moments – which had seemed like a lifetime – it looked like they were all going to drown in the river, separated from one another and on their own.

Out of nowhere, a massive tortoise had slid under JoJo and lifted her safely to the surface, at least enough to breath easily. Next, a woman appeared swimming right next to her. At first, JoJo had thought it to be a mermaid. "Why not, right?" But the woman turned out to have legs after all. She said her name was Yama, and that she was Estrilli, a water-elf. JoJo assumed the Estrilli to be part of the Pure Folk, because that was the only way her brain was going to make all of this work. Yama proceeded to tell her that the Fast Turtles would transport her and her companions rapidly to their destination, wherever along the river that might be. That was how JoJo found out that Marcy and Trip were both safe. She had verified it with her own eyes shortly thereafter.

"Do you ever think about how we're going to tell our friends about this stuff?" Marcy asked a while after JoJo had finished catching her up on how they'd been rescued. They were peacefully cruising through the water, each of them creating their own wakes as they sped down the river. There was no sign of men on horseback trying to keep up with them. The turtles were apparently very fast, indeed.

"What the heck would we say?" JoJo answered with her own question. "I mean, where would you even start? The Leprechaun? Warlock? Talking spiders? Fast Turtles? No one's going to believe *any* of it."

"That's the reason I think we should just keep our mouths shut," Trip joined in. "It's one thing if *you* guys tell these stories since everyone knows you're both smart, but I'd end up getting put away because they'd all think I hit my head on the ice one too many times, and that would be the end of my hockey career."

Marcy looked over at him with a big smile, thinking that Trip was being funny. When she saw how serious he looked, she realized that he wasn't joking around. She glanced at JoJo, who was nodding in confirmation. *Are you telling me that the dumb Jock actually looks at* himself *as dumb?* She'd always seen athletes like Trip strutting around school like peacocks, as if their abilities on the field or court or ice carried over into the classroom, and just assumed that they weren't aware of how little they really knew. *Who's being the peacock now?* she scolded herself silently. She was glad the others couldn't see how red her face had turned.

Yama reappeared after a while, this time accompanied by another of the fascinating water-elves. She gave her name as Vili, and her shocking red hair and face-full of freckles was in sharp contrast to Yama's olive skin and jet-black hair. The Estrilli swam between the tortoises, such that Yama split Trip and JoJo while Vili was right between JoJo and Marcy. They had no problem matching the speed of the Fast Turtles, even though they swam mostly with just their legs.

"How far do you seek to go?" Yama asked, her question apparently aimed at JoJo.

"Camelot," she answered, biting her lip, "or Shadowrock, or whatever you want to call it." Saying the forbidden name reminded her to check if the fake LifeStone was still attached to her ear, which it was. She looked to see the water-elf's reaction.

Yama's face darkened noticeably and her brow furrowed with wrinkles that none of them would have thought possible. "It is a bad place. We choose not to name it at all. What evil calls you there?"

"It's not evil that calls us. It's my Dad. They're holding him prisoner and we're going to bust him out."

"You go openly to confront the darkness of that foul place?" It was Vili's turn to ask a question. Her eyes were wide with astonishment. "How do you expect to succeed?"

"Well..." JoJo pressed her lips together and looked from Trip to Marcy. "We're not really sure. Once we get there, we've sorta got a map to find what we need to trade for my Dad. It's not much of a plan, I know."

"That's an understatement," Trip said laughing. "We don't have a clue. We're probably going to end up in the same dungeon that we're trying to get your dad out of. I just hope they've got a prison hockey team..."

"Very funny, puck-head. And besides, we do have a clue, assuming Marcy's still got it and it hasn't been ruined. And that she can figure it out for us."

The Estrilli listened to this exchange with both amusement and concern. To the water-elves these strange children had an energy about them that was uncommon among the people that they'd come into contact with. Most inhabitants of Erristan led lives of drudgery, with no spark to their actions nor any twinkle in their eyes. Any zest for life that they might have once enjoyed had been thoroughly stomped out by the suffocating control of the dark powers that ruled the land. *And these three youngsters were going to march right up to evil's front door and demand freedom for the girl's father?* Impressive, but it had tragedy written all over it in the eyes of Yama and Vili.

"Will you stay with us all the way to Cam... the city?" Marcy asked the water-elves. She felt for the map, rolled up and tucked away in an inside pocket of her vest, making sure that she hadn't lost it. Relieved by its presence, she continued, "Of course, you're also welcome to go in there with us. The more the merrier."

Yama looked at her gravely. "I sadly regret that we cannot accompany you inside that fell place. It is not a choice for Vili and I to make. Our people have not fared well within the walls of the witches over the ages. As a result, our leaders have forbidden us from attempting to do so ever again."

"Gee, I'm really sorry to hear that," JoJo said, part of her curious about what had happened to the water-elves that hadn't 'fared well' and another part disappointed by Yama's announcement. They could use all the help that they could get.

"The news is worse yet, I'm afraid," Yama continued. She looked down the river, as if she were searching for something. The others followed her line of sight. In the distance, the outlines of a small mountain appeared, seemingly right above the water.

"What's that?" Trip asked, impatient for the Estrilli to explain. "Does the river end there or something?"

"No, it does not *end*," Vili answered softly, "but it changes as it continues under the mountain of the Gnomes. The Estrilli swim those waters with extreme caution, but we pass through freely nonetheless. The same cannot be said of the Fast Turtles. They will not enter the mountain."

JoJo bit her lip as she digested this latest twist. At the speed the turtles were moving, they would cover that distance in little time.

"What're our choices when we get there? I mean, how far do we still have to go to get to you-know-where?"

"From the other side of the mountain – where the Crystalline River exits – it is not far, a short swim for the Estrilli. I cannot imagine it taking that long even for the land-walkers," Yama replied. "Your challenge will clearly be getting around the mountain."

She went on to describe how the King's Road at that point bent away from the river, around the wide base of the mountain, before angling back to rejoin the Crystalline on the other side. They would be easily detained if they attempted to climb out of the river on the Road side prior to the mountain. Trying to circumvent the mountain in the other direction would require a strenuous ascent over rock-strewn slopes, a challenge for the most experienced climbers that would still take more than a day. That was time they didn't have.

"Well, I guess we'll just have to stay in the water and ride it on through," JoJo said finally. She saw the horror, not only in Marcy's eyes but also in those of the water-elves. Trip smiled and shrugged his shoulders. "I mean, seriously, what choice do we have?"

"You could have asked how the rest of us feel about it," Marcy snapped. *"How in the world are we supposed to survive the river without the Fast Turtles?* Not to mention, Yama and Vili here are white as ghosts now."

"I'm sorry, Marcy. I really am. But honestly, I don't see any other option. If you've got an idea that won't cost us an extra day that we don't have, and won't put us right in the hands of the Black Wind, then I'm all for it. Otherwise, we're just going to have to trust that our new friends here will keep us from drowning inside that mountain."

"That will be the least of your concerns," Vili said solemnly.

Chapter Twenty-three

Fish or Cut Bait

The mountain loomed menacingly ahead as they felt the tortoises slow down noticeably. The sun wasn't yet at its midpoint in the sky, casting shadows over most of this side of the mountain, including the large cave-like opening that seemed to swallow the river. Yama and Vili were nowhere in sight, having swum off earlier without a word.

"This does *not* look good," Marcy announced, hoping that she could convince JoJo to change her mind. "I almost drowned once today *already*, JoJo. This is simply going to finish the job. And if the Fast Turtles are too scared to go in there, what makes you think we should?"

"Because of them," Trip answered, even though the question wasn't directed exactly at him. He was pointing off to the right, where the King's Road began to turn away from the river. Barely visible in the shadows were seven men in black cloaks, sitting atop their equally dark horses. Waiting.

"They couldn't be the same ones," JoJo wondered aloud. "How many of these dang patrols are there, anyway?"

The resistance of the water against their bodies reversed direction as the Fast Turtles came to a virtual stop twenty yards from the cave entrance. Now the river's current flowed past them from behind as they sat still in the water, contemplating how to accomplish what they needed to do next.

"We can't just jump off and swim for it," Trip said, staring at the massive opening into which the river disappeared. "Not with all these clothes on. If we had something like that barrel to hang onto, then we could just ride the current on through, know what I mean?"

"Yeah, well if we had a nice boat, we could drink ice coffee and eat Pop-Tarts while we cruised on down. Maybe even sit back with our fishing poles and catch a mackerel or two," JoJo replied, scowling at Trip. She knew he was speaking both his mind and the truth, but she needed help in convincing Marcy that they could do this, not more reasons why they couldn't.

Surprisingly, the tortoises did nothing to urge them to dismount, seemingly content to tread water while their three passengers made up their minds. Likewise, the Black Wind on the bank made no apparent move to force their hand, patient to wait for these strange children to make their way to land. The ball was obviously in JoJo's court, but she couldn't seem to execute the decision she'd already made.

"Okay listen," she said, biting her lip. "When we jump in, Marcy needs to be in the middle so that Trip and I can each keep a hand on her, okay? With any luck, the current will shoot us through there in no time, and we'll hook up with some other turtles or something on the other side. You guys with me?"

Trip nodded, no differently than if a hockey coach had just told him that he had ten seconds to go in and skate through six defenders and score the game-winning goal. Piece of cake. Marcy, on the other hand, was pale. Paler than normal. Her wide eyes betrayed any show of confidence in the others' ability to keep her alive. She tried to slow her breathing and get her racing heart under control.

"Okay, on three," JoJo said, trying to sound as encouraging as she could for Marcy's sake. "One, two…"

"Hold it!" Trip interrupted, reaching over to stop Marcy from jumping. Pointing toward the dark cave opening, he asked, "What's that?"

Coming toward them on the water's surface was a pile of driftwood, all seemingly tangled together. It wouldn't have been considered all that odd a sight for the river except that it was coming *upstream.* As it made its way closer, it became apparent that the pile was aiming right at them. If the Fast Turtles were aware of it, they made no move to get out of the way.

"Hey!" Marcy squeaked, bracing for the collision. Although she wasn't about to voluntarily abandon ship, she hoped her tortoise would do something to keep her from being run over. She put her hands out in front of her, locking her elbows and stiffening her legs for the impact.

It never came. The tangle of wood came to a stop a few feet short of Marcy and the others. It took her a few moments to realize that she was holding her breath, and that it was probably okay to blow it out and relax her limbs. She jumped when a head popped up out of the water next to the drift-pile. A spray of water flew from flaming red hair as Vili shook her head from side to side. Her freckled smile beamed above the surface.

From the other side, Yama's appearance was marked by the stream of water that came from her long black hair whipping around. Unlike her companion, she was not smiling. In fact, she was practically scowling.

"Although I do not approve of your intention," she announced to JoJo, "we will endeavor to assist you as we can. This raft will not support your combined weight, but might be strong enough for one of you to ride atop. More importantly, it will give you something to hold onto while you negotiate the river through the mountain."

"Just like the barrel, eh JoJo?" Trip said, laughing out loud. "Only way better."

JoJo no longer bit her lip. This was exactly what they needed. She hoped. Looking from one of the Estrilli to the other, she asked, "Are you guys going to be with us all the way through?"

"That is our intention," Vili answered, still perkier than her elf-sister. "Unless, of course…"

"What?" Marcy jumped in. "Unless what? Are you expecting trouble in there?"

Yama looked to be upset at the red-headed water-elf. Turning to face Marcy and JoJo she indicated the mountain with her head. "That is the home of the Gnomes, as I have already told you. The worst mistake anyone entering the mountain can make is to *not* expect trouble. The Gnomes are not fond of outsiders, to say the least. Even the corrupted Half-locks are hesitant to step foot inside that domain."

JoJo followed Yama's eyes to the Black Wind leader sitting on his horse on the riverbank. A shiver ran down her spine, even though the magical servant of the Gories didn't appear to be doing anything at that moment.

"How come you guys aren't afraid?" Trip asked curiously. "I mean, why don't the Gnomes bother you?"

"The Estrilli are mostly friends of all the Pure Folk, including the Gnomes. Nevertheless, the small men think that everyone who enters their mountain does so to steal from them. It doesn't help that that has indeed been the case on too many occasions. In the eyes and minds of the Gnomes, it is better to be vigilant against all, rather than try to keep track of allies and enemies. That said, we must not give them *any* reason to think we wish to do *anything* more than quickly pass through the mountain."

"Well, I think we better get going then," JoJo said, jerking her thumb toward the shore. "Those guys look like they're getting ready to do something that we probably won't like."

A small rowboat was being lowered into the water just in front of where the Black Wind horses stomped anxiously. Two of the cloaked men had already dismounted and were getting ready to join a pair of oarsmen in the boat. Apparently, they meant to come out and fetch JoJo and her friends right out of the middle of the river.

Vili ducked her head underwater, and JoJo thought she could actually hear the water-elf talking. When she came back above the surface, Marcy began to rise higher and higher in the water. The smartest sixth-grader at Mahoney Middle School was almost as scared as if she had been going in the opposite direction. Almost.

"That is to make it easier for you to climb onto the raft," Vili said as she and Yama pushed the driftwood closer. When she noticed Marcy's hesitation, she added urgency to her tone, "Please hurry!"

Marcy clumsily leaned forward, letting her knees make contact with the tangle of wood first before bending and reaching with her hands. Grabbing tightly to branches that had somehow been woven together, she lifted her feet from the back of her tortoise and climbed on her hands and knees until she was in the approximate center of the makeshift raft.

JoJo and Trip looked at one another and they both nodded. Finding good branches to hold onto, they pushed forward in the water simultaneously, leaving the Fast Turtles free to move away from the entrance to the dastardly mountain. Almost immediately, the floating collection of driftwood began moving swiftly toward the giant opening.

The rowboat was not attempting to come straight at them, but rather was angling in such a way as to cut them off before entering the cave. The two oarsmen strained to pull the boat through the cross-current, urged on by the Black Wind with them, one Tracker and one Assassin. At this speed and angle, they would have no problem intercepting the slow-moving pile of branches.

Suddenly, JoJo felt the raft lurch forward. She looked at Trip and saw him grit his teeth and tighten his grip. Just as she made sure that she wasn't going to lose her hold on the branch, it seemed like the raft shifted into another gear. Not only was there no need for

JoJo and Trip to kick their feet to assist in propelling the craft

forward – there was no opportunity for them to do so. Their legs

trailed straight behind them on the surface as they sped down the

river.

It was all JoJo could do to keep her face above the water.

Otherwise, she wouldn't have seen them race into the dark cave

opening a mere boat-length ahead of the rowboat.

Chapter Twenty-four

Gnome Sweet Gnome

"Hey, I thought you said they were too scared to come in here!" Marcy shout-whispered at Yama and Vili while she pointed with her eyes at the rowboat behind them. "They're going to catch us!"

Water splashed up into her face as the makeshift raft picked up speed.

"They cannot catch us unless we wish to be caught," Vili said cheerfully. Marcy could barely make her face out in the darkness of the vast cavern. Looking back, she could see the rowboat falling further and further behind, the light outside the cave making it easy to spot.

"Besides, they have larger concerns than trying to catch up to us," Yama added from the other side of the raft. Neither of the Estrilli appeared to be exerting much effort as they propelled the tangled pile of branches down the river. JoJo and Trip, on the other hand, were hanging on for dear life as they trailed along at the back end of the driftwood, struggling to keep their heads up and the rushing water out of their mouths. Neither of them could even begin to look back over their shoulders at whatever was going on with their pursuers.

Marcy saw one of the standing figures in the rowboat fall over and splash into the water, as if she had thunked him in the head with a stone from her sling-shot. Only she hadn't even taken it out of her pocket, so she knew it wasn't her. Before she could figure out what had happened, the second cloaked man standing in the boat toppled over the edge, swallowed by the dark river. The boat slowed immediately, turning sharply to head back the way it had come.

"Did the Gnomes do that?" Marcy asked the water-elves, turning her head from one to the other. Instead of an answer, she felt the raft move even faster. Although she worried for JoJo and Trip, she was entirely thankful that she wasn't hanging on to the back end of this bundle of floating sticks going ninety miles an hour downriver in complete darkness. She decided to watch for any signs that they would be next on the Gnomes' target list.

The light from where they'd entered faded into a small speck while there was no sign of the exit at the other end. Increasingly, they approached utter blackness. Maybe it was for this reason that the Estrilli slowed down, perhaps afraid of blindly running into something that would either hurt them or offend someone else. JoJo didn't know and didn't care. She was just happy to have a chance to pull her chest up onto the raft for a breather, giving her tired arms a much-needed rest. She figured that Trip was doing the same by the way the back end of the driftwood pile was tilting downward, deeper into the water.

"You okay?" she whispered hoarsely to him.

"Yeah great," he answered sarcastically. "We ought to make it a point to do this once a week or so."

JoJo laughed out loud, and was immediately *Shh'd!* by both of the water-elves and Marcy. The laughter and the reprimands alike echoed off the unseen ceiling of the humongous cavern. Soon, the only sound was that of the driftwood raft lightly splashing through the water.

"What are those blue lights?" Trip asked after a while, careful to keep his voice low.

JoJo and Marcy strained to see what he was talking about before they were both able to pick out the tiny specks of intense blue light scattered along the walls and ceiling that surrounded the river. The lights twinkled on and off and appeared to move, never staying in the same places for more than an instant. They looked almost like a disorganized collection of very small, blue Christmas lights, blinking against the blackness.

"Do not look!" Yama cautioned in a hoarse whisper. "Those are the FireGems of the mountain, the very precious reason that the Gnomes guard this place so zealously. Do not give them reason to think that you covet what is theirs."

They did as they were told, although JoJo wondered how anyone could tell what she was looking at in the darkness of the cavern. Trip was only four feet away from her, and she couldn't see in what direction he was looking, so how…

Thud!

Marcy screamed, and the driftwood raft shuddered.

Thud! Thud!

More shrieking from Marcy pierced the vastness of the river cavern. JoJo slid off of the back end of the raft and almost lost her grip. She tried to see what was causing all the commotion, but all she could make out were shadows moving in the blackness. Small shadows.

"Bring this craft to the docks," barked a sharp voice from the middle of the raft, right about where Marcy should have been. The voice reminded JoJo of the Munchkin people, which normally would have made her laugh, but things didn't appear to be all that funny right now.

She felt the driftwood lurch dramatically to her right and guessed that the water-elves were responsible. The back end of the raft rose slightly and she sensed that Trip had also pushed himself off of the raft and back into the water. The river's current now nudged at them from the side, causing her legs to trail off to the left. She thought she felt Trip's foot poke her in the ribs once or twice.

Suddenly, her legs dropped straight below her and she hung limply from the branches that she grasped. The current was gone and their makeshift raft was no longer moving. She wished she could see past the tip of her nose.

Feet slapping on stone close to her gave some indication that they were near a solid flat surface, and also that they were far from alone. JoJo felt small – *very small* – hands grab her arms and surprisingly lift her out of the water.

"Hey! What the…?" Trip said, more scared than anything else as he was also pulled out of the water. JoJo remembered the previous Halloween when the two of them had gone to a haunted house together. He had not been a big fan of all the unseen things touching him in the darkness at that time, either. Then again, neither was she.

"Trip? JoJo? Where are you guys?" Marcy sounded as meek as a human could be, on the verge of tears. She seemed to still be in the middle of the raft... "Eeek! What *is* that? Something's touching me! Oh, oh, oh, *oh*!"

They were standing on a flat section of rock, the best that JoJo could tell. She reached her hands out in Marcy's direction, making contact and pulling her close. "We're right here. You're okay."

"*Okay*? Are you out of your mind?" Marcy was sounding almost delirious. "We can't even see each other in this pitch-black, and little paws or claws keep grabbing at me. There is nothing 'okay' about this!"

"Quiet!" the sharp Munchkin voice ordered from knee-level, echoing off the water and stone. "You elves must remain here until we return, or depart as you wish. These others will come with us."

Unseen tiny hands began pushing the three children in their legs, directing them which way to go in the blackness. *How can these guys see?* JoJo wondered to herself. She'd been in the dark before, and understood the basics of night vision and how her eyes could adjust pretty well if given enough time, but this just seemed like another kind of darkness altogether. She held her arms out, moving them from her front to her sides, trying to make sure she didn't smack into a wall or something worse. Her hands found Trip's back, who was apparently right in front of her. Likewise, she felt what she hoped were Marcy's hands poking her from behind.

As they were herded along, the sound of the water lapping against the stone dock was replaced by occasional dripping. JoJo guessed that they were walking through a tunnel of some kind, swearing that she could barely start to see shadows in the darkness. The outline of Trip's head and shoulders were a different shade of dark than the space immediately surrounding him, and she also was pretty sure she could make out wet glistening stone walls to their sides. Every now and then they were told to lower their heads for a while, which she assumed had to do with lower ceilings. Whoever was pushing on her legs certainly didn't need a very high open space to walk through, she mused silently, so these tunnels probably weren't made for regular people. As they veered sharply to their

right, she saw a glow straight ahead.

Trip, JoJo and Marcy stumbled out of the tunnel into a large

chamber the size of their school library. It was faintly lit by glowing

piles of luminescent rocks placed at intervals around the room. The

light was just enough for them to see that the walls and ceiling were

nothing fancier than chiseled stone, with occasional rivulets of water

running down to the floor and disappearing through unseen cracks.

In the center of the chamber was an immense short-legged granite

table, the ends of which each held a huge bowl of the glowing rocks.

Centered between the bowls was a fancy chair that looked about the

size of one that JoJo used to have for her large dolls. Sitting lazily in

the chair was a tiny little man.

JoJo looked down all around her just then, and confirmed

that the small hands that had been guiding her to this point all

belonged to similarly tiny people. They all wore hard-looking round

helmets with little horns sticking out of them, reminding her of

miniature Vikings. She couldn't make out all of their facial features,

but it appeared that most had beards and moustaches and muscular hairy arms. Their clothing consisted of drab cut-off pants and sleeveless vests dominated by a wide belt with a prominent buckle in the middle. No doubt, these were the Gnomes. *Geez*, she thought, *I hope none of these are women.*

"What brings you to my mountain?" the man in the chair – apparently his throne – asked with a self-important air. "Do you not know that *thieves* are unwelcome here?"

"Who are you calling *thieves*?" JoJo answered with her own question. She didn't steal from anyone – anymore – and resented the accusation. "We're just passing through. You know, a short-cut on our way to Camelot?"

A collective suction of breath echoed through the chamber. "Take *care* how you address King Odnil, greatest among the Gnomes of earth," the one who had led them here from the docks warned. At least, JoJo thought it was the same one.

"The time for caution has passed," the King announced. "Now is the time for payment."

Chapter Twenty-five

King Odnil

JoJo, Marcy and Trip looked at one another in the muted light. All around them, Gnomes cheered and slapped their bare feet on the stone floor, excited by their King's pronouncement. *They need to get cable TV or something down here*, JoJo thought to herself as she watched the celebration. She stared at King Odnil, who appeared to be more than satisfied with himself.

"We really don't have anything to pay you with," JoJo answered when the hooting and hollering had died down somewhat. "Look, we're just trying to get to the castle – you know, Camelot or Shadowrock or whatever you want to call it? – and get my Dad out of there. Believe it or not, we're not even *from* here."

The King arched an eyebrow in amusement. The other Gnomes remained silent, smiling broadly and waiting for his response. Apparently, they had all seen this game played out before with other 'guests'. These strangers were about to find out that no one passes through the mountain without cost. If you couldn't afford the payment, you were best off going around or over the mountain. Some who entered the home of the Gnomes were not even given the opportunity to offer tribute to the King because of past bad blood, such as the Black Wind. True, if enough Half-locks were able to gain entrance under the mountain, they could wreak havoc on the little people, but the effort was not worth the price to them. Not yet, anyway. Because of a centuries-old agreement, only the Estrilli were granted free passage in the river waters that ran through here. And that did *not* include any companions that the water-elves may have in their company.

"Perhaps you have more to offer than you are revealing?" the King responded, rubbing his tiny hands together.

"Look, she's telling the truth," Trip interrupted, a little too sharply for the tastes of the Gnomes. There were more than a few gasps in the crowd. He ignored them and pulled his pants pockets inside-out. "See? Nothing. We don't have a penny on us."

JoJo followed Trip's example and pulled the insides of her pockets out as well. Marcy searched her long skirt for pockets and found none. Instead, she pulled her vest open to show that she wasn't hiding anything. Too late, she realized that she was indeed carrying something in a pocket inside her vest, giving the impression that it was valuable enough to conceal. The map.

"What have we here?" King Odnil asked, pointing a small bony finger at the rolled-up sheepskin sticking out of the top of the vest pocket. "Bring that to me!"

Marcy closed her vest and took a step back, as if she'd just been physically assaulted. Little hands pushed against her legs, shoving her toward the throne. She looked helplessly at JoJo, who shrugged her shoulders and motioned for her to cooperate.

"Let him take a look at it," JoJo said, matter-of-factly and as if the King wasn't even in the room. "Maybe he can help us make some sense out of that gibberish written on there. As long as he gives it back when he's done looking at it." She didn't care that this earned her a glare from the Gnome ruler.

Marcy stopped in front of the center of the table, reached into her vest and removed the map. Her hand shook as she extended the rolled-up sheepskin to Odnil, who snatched it away greedily. She immediately retreated a few steps, not wanting to be any closer to this ridiculously powerful little man than she absolutely had to.

The map seemed enormous in the tiny hands of the King as he disappeared behind the unrolled document. It was difficult for JoJo and her friends to know what he thought of it because they could neither see most of his body nor make out what he was mumbling on the other side of the map. After a few moments, he rolled it up but made no effort to offer it back to Marcy. He looked at both girls, seemingly dismissing Trip as not important in this discussion.

"Where did you get this?" Odnil asked seriously. The question had an ominous tone that had been missing earlier. No other Gnome in the room made a noise.

"It was in a hole in our basement wall behind Stonewall Jackson," JoJo answered, trying to take some of the gravity out of the discussion. When no one laughed, she continued, "Why? What's the matter?"

King Odnil stared at her in silence for what seemed a very long time. Finally, he held the map roll up, as if she might not know what he was talking about. "Understand that we Gnomes are long-lived, much more so than frail humans or many other beings of this world. We measure our ages by the wear of the rock inside this mountain rather than the passing of the seasons, and I have seen much stone worn away by the river. Yet this map is old. Older even than I am, or my father, or his father before him. So, I ask you again, how come you by it?"

This time, JoJo knew better than to offer up a wise-crack. There was no joking in the King's tone, nor did there appear to be any tolerance for it. She looked at her friends for any sign of encouragement, but all they could offer were shrugs of their shoulders.

"My Dad left it for us… for me. I don't know how he got it, but a couple of people have told me that he was a Free Knight in this world before he became my Dad in our world. I don't know what to believe any more. We don't have Gnomes and water-elves and Leprechauns where we come from, so all of this is really weird for me and my friends. All I know is that that map is supposed to lead us to something that will help free my Dad from the Gories. You know, the witches?"

"What 'something' would that be?" Odnil asked, leaning forward. "The witches strike no *easy* bargains, and almost never relinquish their prisoners unless the price is extravagantly high. So, tell me – what is it you seek in the old castle?"

At this rate, by the time we get there this is going to be the worst-kept secret in the history of secrets, JoJo told herself as she wrung her hands nervously in front of her. And bit her lip. She cleared her throat before answering.

"There's this thing called a *Chrimeus*, and apparently…"

"I know what you speak of," he cut her off sharply. Waving the map at her, he asked, "And you think this will help you find it?"

"That's what we're hoping," Trip said, surprisingly stepping in to take some of the pressure off of his best buddy. "We brought the brainiac along to solve the riddle-puzzle thing, so it shouldn't be a problem. You're not saying that the map's a fake, are you?"

The King was shocked by the utter lack of respect shown by these humans. Although they seemed young, even for their kind, they still should be able to demonstrate a minimum level of courtesy. At least, that was his way of viewing it. He looked at the boy as if Trip had just slapped him.

"Do *not* speak out of turn," Odnil ordered acidly, "or you will never see the outside of this mountain again, much less the inside of Camelot. I would not think twice to reward your insolence with a lifetime of acting as a target for our hunting games. Is that understood?"

Trip started to answer, but then wasn't sure if he was even supposed to do *that*, so he just nodded his head and mumbled "whatever" under his breath. *If I had my hockey stick right now,* he thought silently, *this guy would be a puck on the receiving end of my slap-shot.* Then *we could talk about 'games'.*

"He didn't mean anything rude by it," JoJo defended. "What he said was the same as what would've come out of my mouth, pretty much. Marcy here is our best chance for figuring out what those codes mean on the side. *Is* there something wrong with the map?"

King Odnil eyed her for a moment. Thankfully, the light wasn't good enough to see his eyes clearly because they would have made JoJo uncomfortable in a creepy way. Finally, he seemed to have come to a conclusion in his own mind. He sat back in his little throne and tapped the map against his knee several times.

"This map was drawn *before* the fall of Camelot," he began, sounding more like a history teacher now. "Whatever clues are embedded in the map itself may not be valid any longer, given that it's been more than a thousand years since naive Arthur was defeated. Except for one thing. These 'puzzles', as you call them, have been added recently, sometime in the past hundred years. That means that the *Chrimeus* was placed somewhere in Shadowrock not all that long ago. If your Free Knight father had this, it is also quite probable that he either hid the *Chrimeus* himself or was given it by whoever did stash the Marble."

"Marble? What do you mean?" Marcy asked. For some reason, Odnil did not seem as offended by her as he had been when Trip asked questions uninvited.

"The Five Marbles," he replied, looking straight at her. "The *Chrimeus* is one of them. Supposedly, it was given to Merlin, and from it he drew most of his legendary magical ability. Without the *Chrimeus*, Merlin would have been no more than a cheap apothecary, mixing potions to remove warts and solve stomach pains."

"That would explain why Beglis wants it," JoJo said, thinking out loud. "And the Gories."

"You will give the *Chrimeus* to neither the forest warlock nor the witches," Kind Odnil announced standing up. "The Gories would never feel compelled to honor any bargain once they have such a powerful talisman, and there would be little you could do about it. Nor anyone else, including us. The witches would certainly move to exterminate all the Pure Folk."

JoJo looked uncomfortably at the Gnome ruler. "But how do I save my Dad? I only care about this stupid Marble because that's what they want before they'll let him go."

"That is not my concern," Odnil answered solemnly. "The life of one Free Knight is not worth the entire Gnome kingdom."

Chapter Twenty-Six

Another Bargain

JoJo was stunned.

If they couldn't trade the *Chrimeus* for her Dad, then all their efforts were for nothing. It was already going to be difficult enough, just getting into the fortress and finding the hidden Marble. That was assuming that it was located somewhere on the map, and they could somehow decipher the cryptic clues written on it. Now, it appeared that they weren't even going to get the opportunity to try.

The life of one Free Knight is not worth... The words bounced around inside her skull. *How in the world could he say that? We're talking about my* father, *for Pete's sake!*

"Fine," she said, trying to clear her head and think straight. "We'll just take the map and be on our way, then. Since you're not going to help us."

"I think not," the King replied, pulling the map to his chest like it might be more secure there. "As I said, the *Chrimeus* cannot be allowed to fall into the wrong hands. It is best left hidden as it is."

Marcy raised her hand for permission to speak, as if she were in school. Trip rolled his eyes, but in the half-light of the dimly illuminated chamber no one saw. Odnil tilted his head at Marcy in surprise, and then gestured with his empty hand for her to say what was on her mind.

"Sir," she squeaked, cleared her throat a bit and continued, "what if we agreed not to give the *Chrimeus* to the Gories? Wouldn't you feel better knowing it wasn't right there under their noses where they might find it by accident? We could even bring it back here and you could hide it somewhere in your mountain."

For the first time since they'd entered the large room there was a rumble of Gnome voices all around. Apparently, the idea of the magical Marble residing here among them created quite a stir.

Unfortunately for Marcy and her companions, it wasn't the good kind of excitement.

"Silence!" King Odnil commanded. The result was immediate as the chamber became instantly quiet. The air seemed suddenly thicker than it had been up until now. The Gnome king looked sternly at Marcy. "Such a thing is not possible, child. For one thing, the *Chrimeus* – and all of its sister Marbles – are unnatural creations of Conjured Magic, which cannot coexist with the Pure. For a Gnome or Fairy or Leprechaun to attempt to even handle such a mutation of nature would bring catastrophic results, unpredictable in their form but not their scale. Those not of the Pure have shown themselves to be unreliable when vested with such power, whether man, elf, or dwarf. The Free Knights were given the responsibility of safe-guarding this Marble for that very reason."

"But who are they supposed to be saving it for, then?" Marcy asked, not missing a beat. Whenever logic was involved, she felt she had a distinct advantage. "I mean, is there supposed to be another Merlin coming along that we have to wait a thousand years for? I can understand not wanting the Gories to get their hands on the Marble, but if it stays hidden then they win anyway."

"How do you mean?" Odnil asked, his little eyebrow arched.

"Well, it looks like the Gories have a humongous advantage already because they have serious magic and the Black Wind – not to mention Pewtris Grimm – on their side, while the good guys consist of a handful of Free Knights and the various Pure Folk who don't seem to be able to flex a whole lot of muscle outside of their own backyards. If the *Chrimeus* never comes out of hiding, it can't be used to level the playing field against the witches, so by keeping it buried they continue to win."

There had been a collective gasp when she said Pewtris Grimm's name, as if something bad would come of it. The King seemed totally immersed in Marcy's explanation, his brow furrowed as he digested what she was saying. Trip and JoJo were doing likewise. To both of them, Marcy made perfect sense, but neither of them would have been able to come up with that argument on their own.

"We are not so bad off, as things currently stand," Odnil countered after he'd considered what she said. "The witches leave us alone, and you witnessed what happens when their Black Wind underlings attempt to gain entrance to this mountain."

Marcy wasn't about to let go. She was like a dog with a bone right now, and she could feel that this Gnome king was at least willing to listen to her. "What happens when they decide that they want your FireGems for themselves, or they get tired of itsy-bitsy Gnomes controlling river passage through the mountain? You may be alright for the time being, but as soon as the Gories decide otherwise, you're going to be helpless to stop them. Maybe it would be a good idea to have an ally with the ability to stand up to them?"

"Such as? There hasn't been a wizard capable of harnessing the power of the *Chrimeus* since Merlin perished ten centuries ago." King Odnil crossed his arms as if to signify that there was no acceptable answer to his question. "Certainly, you don't consider the *warlock* to be the least bit qualified to even hold the Marble, much less employ its magicks?"

The thought of Beglis controlling the most powerful magical object known to man sent shivers down Marcy's back. Memories of the slickly-dressed woods wizard forcing them into a deal so that they could get rid of the LifeStones caused the hairs on the back of her neck to rise. Still, it was possible that Beglis was the best choice available…

"What about someone who's not a wizard?" JoJo asked out of the blue. The question caught Odnil off-guard, so she continued. "Is there some rule that says you have to already be a wizard before you can become a wizard? Because if that's the case, then it's a really stupid rule, if you don't mind my saying."

"I must say," King Odnil said as he tried to keep from choking on JoJo's outburst, "that I've never even contemplated such a thing. But I suppose you're correct. Even Merlin wasn't a magician while he was still in his mother's womb, so he had to become one somewhere along the way." He narrowed his gaze at her. "Exactly whom did you have in mind?"

"Why not Marcy?" JoJo offered without warning, jerking her thumb at her friend.

"Why not me *what*?" Marcy sputtered, completely unprepared.

"Oh, come on, Marcy," JoJo urged, trying to communicate with her eyes in the murky light. *Just go with this, will you?* "You're smarter than probably anyone else in this whole kingdom, so you could pick up this... wizardy stuff real easy, I'm sure. I mean, it can't be any harder than all that science and math that you read for fun, right?"

Before Marcy could protest, Trip snapped his head around toward her and interrupted. "Science and math for *fun*? Seriously?"

"Hey, not everyone gets their jollies by slipping around on the ice and swinging a stick, okay?" His teasing jibe had thrown her back into the defensive mode she always relied on whenever other kids made fun of her love of academics. Especially Jocks. Turning back to JoJo and King Odnil, she continued, "What if I don't *want* to do it?"

Trip was not so easily ignored. "For someone so smart you sure do sound... *not* so smart. Dude, you've got a chance to be as magical as Merlin – maybe even better – and you don't '*want*' that? What the heck's wrong with you?"

"Not *everyone* is all about fame and glory, you know?" Marcy squeezed the words out of her mouth, slowly and deliberately. "I've worked hard for every scrap of knowledge that has made its way into my head. This... this Marble or *Chrimeus* or whatever you want to call it would be like cheating. It's not *earned*, and I don't ever want anyone to be able to say that about me or anything I ever accomplish. Maybe you can't understand that since your talent is all natural."

"Natural? I work my *butt* off to be better than everyone else," Trip answered through clenched teeth. "You have no idea what real hard work..."

"Enough!" It was JoJo who cut him off, seeing their opportunity slipping away. "*I'll* do it. I'll be the next wizard or whatever you want to call me. I'll make sure that the *Chrimeus* doesn't end up in the wrong hands."

King Odnil looked at JoJo as if her were appraising a work of art or a prize pig. Indeed, what was running through his mind was much more important than beauty or the quality of pork. After a long pause, he asked, "What assurances do I have that you will not attempt to exchange the Marble for your father after all?"

"Because what you said earlier makes sense. The Gories are never going to let any of us go after we give them the *Chrimeus*. We've all seen enough movies to know that the bad guys always double-cross you in the end." She took a deep breath before continuing. "So… if you help us free my Dad, then you have my word about the Marble."

The King surprised everyone in the chamber when he burst out laughing. The sound was even stranger than his talking voice, and Trip was trying his hardest to keep from breaking into his own laughter. Marcy was, as usual, worried that JoJo's proposal was so ridiculous that they were probably now headed to the Gnome dungeons.

"Great minds seem to think alike," Odnil said when he finally composed himself. "I had every intention of sending a team of my very best Gnomes to accompany you on this mission. They will serve to guide you, assist in freeing your father, and ensure that you do the correct thing with the *Chrimeus*. If you betray me, they will end your quest most unpleasantly."

Chapter Twenty-Seven

The Back Door

They didn't come out the same way they entered. Once it had been decided, King Odnil provided them with a collection of Gnomes under the command of his most trusted lieutenant, whose name was Ulnick. Word had been sent to the waiting Estrilli to go ahead and depart without their new friends; they wouldn't be rejoining them. Instead, JoJo and her two best buddies in the world were led through a series of tunnels that climbed through the mountain and took them over the river to the other side. Thankfully, a couple of the Gnomes carried small containers of the glowing rocks, enabling the three middle-schoolers to keep from bumping into the low ceilings or sharp outcroppings from the rock walls.

"How many people are you going to promise that... you-know-what to?" Marcy whispered to JoJo as they walked. "Someone's not going to be very happy!"

"I'm working on it," JoJo mumbled back to her. "One thing at a time, okay?"

She had already been contemplating the same thing, ever since the words left her mouth promising that she'd take care of the *Chrimeus*. Of course, Beglis would be expecting his payment, and he didn't seem like someone they wanted to get crosswise with. Anyone who could free them of the Gories' magical earrings probably knew a few other tricks as well. However, she hadn't had time to think about that in King Odnil's throne room. She had felt the opportunity to save Dad slipping away, and grabbed hold of the only thing that meant anything to the Gnome king. She'd have to deal with the warlock later. If they made it that far.

The daylight was almost blinding when they made their way out of the tunnel. Luckily, the last stretch inside the mountain had enabled their eyes to start adjusting as the light made its way into the passageway for a little while before they actually exited. Nonetheless, JoJo and her friends squinted and shielded their eyes from the brightness of day when they stepped out onto the rocky slopes on the mountain's far side.

"Someone want to tell me the plan?" Trip said, following Marcy out of the tunnel. They could hear the river off to their right, but it wasn't visible from where they were standing. "I'm still not sure what's going on with all these tiny midgets."

JoJo chuckled, despite the seriousness of their situation. "Well, according to Ulnick, it isn't all that far to Camelot from here, and we're better off walking over on this side of the river where we can't be seen. If we tried to get back in the water, we'd be spotted long before we ever got to the castle. And the King's Road is obviously a no-go. As far as all these Gnomes go, the way I understand it is we've got guys who are fighters, others who know the inside of Shadowrock, and a couple of wicked smart little fellas who can help us try to figure out what the clues on the map say. So, we get in, find the Marble, rescue Dad, and get the heck back out. Same as before, but now we have to figure out some way to trick the witches into freeing Dad without giving them what they want. Piece of cake."

"I don't know, JoJo," he mused aloud, seemingly serious. "Am I going to have to miss another day of skating for this?"

The trail was narrow for humans, but seemed plenty wide for the tiny Gnomes. They walked in single file with Ulnick in the lead and a couple of soldier-Gnomes right behind him. JoJo and her friends were next, followed by the rest of the entourage. Because the path twisted left-and-right and up-and-down with plenty of rocks to either side, it was difficult for her to get an accurate count of how many there were in their group, but she figured it had to be a couple of dozen, at a minimum.

JoJo was mainly interested in the soldiers and whether they would actually be able to help free her Dad if it came down to fighting. Although they certainly looked fierce enough in their little helmets and various weapons, they were just so... *small*. At most, they came up to her knees. She couldn't imagine these miniature warriors doing all that much harm to regular full-sized fighting men like the Black Wind. *Then again...*, she thought to herself.

"Hey Ulnick," she said in an almost conversational tone. "What happened to those guys in the boat that chased us into the mountain?"

He turned his head but kept on walking. "They were targeted by our archers. Actually, it was more like archery practice for our novices, given how big and slow-moving the targets were. Those rowing the boat were allowed to depart unharmed. We Gnomes recognize that the oarsmen do not desire to enter the mountain, and were only doing so at sword-point."

"How many of those archers did you bring with us?" Marcy asked hopefully.

"Enough," he answered, "to start and finish a small war." Ulnick must have considered the matter settled because he returned his attention to his front and said nothing more.

The sun was now on the other side of the mountain, casting long shadows as they continued along the stony trail. Occasionally, they would catch glimpses of the river to their right as the path meandered closer to the water for brief periods of time. For the most part, however, they were not visible to anyone searching from the far side of the Crystalline.

"What's that?" Trip asked, interrupting the crunching of their shoes on the gravel. JoJo and Marcy looked up and strained to see what he was pointing at. Not very far away were high black walls that disappeared into dark clouds.

"That would be Shadowrock, boy." Ulnick looked over his shoulder. His Munchkin-like voice was a bit gruffer than the others, and his tone said that the answer was obvious to all. Trip's face heated at the notion of being treated like he was stupid, but he held his tongue. The Gnome didn't seem to care.

"Aren't they going to see us coming?" JoJo asked, staring up at the walls, looking for any sign that they were being watched. The tops of the walls and towers were lost in the thick charcoal-colored fog that hung over the fortress.

"We will not give them that opportunity," Ulnick answered curtly. Without warning, they left the trail and turned sharply to the left between two large rocks that seem to jut straight up from the ground. While the Gnomes passed easily through the gap, there was barely enough space for JoJo and her friends to follow.

The passageway they now found themselves in resembled a crack in the rough terrain that made up this side of the river. If they thought that the trail had been narrow, they were really squeezed for space now, as the rocky sides scraped at their arms and hips. Luckily, they didn't have to duck because the fissure extended all the way up to the darkening sky. Winding lazily left and right, the passageway disappeared quickly around a sharp right-hand turn. Ulnick stopped here as the group closed up on each other.

"This is where we enter the fortress from," he announced to JoJo and her companions. "Long before the fall of Arthur and Merlin, it was deemed a good strategic idea to create a secret way into Camelot in case there was ever need. That need has seldom arisen, especially since the occupation of the castle by the witches and their lackeys. However, King Odnil has dispatched me on occasion to make sure that access was still available, and to make brief reconnaissance of the happenings within. It is a distasteful place, whatever it once was. Nevertheless, we are about to enter tunnels that were not created for humans, even ones not quite fully grown. As such, you will encounter extremely tight passages along the way. You cannot let these stop you."

Marcy groaned at the thought. She'd already considered the spaces they had been squeezing through to be pretty tight. If he was warning them about worse to come, she wasn't sure how far she could make it. Looking past Ulnick, she saw a small cave-like opening in the rock face. *Great,* she complained to herself, *I've got to duck already. I can only imagine this* not *getting better.* There was a ledge of stone overhanging the entrance like an awning, making the secret doorway practically invisible unless you were right here in front of it. One of the Gnomes handed her a smooth stone that was cool to the touch.

"It is a glow-rock," he explained as he gave one to each of her companions as well, "to help you see in the tunnels."

"Too bad we don't have one of those head-lamps," Trip said, tossing the fist-sized stone up and down lightly. "But I guess this is better than smacking our heads in the pitch-dark, right?"

Marcy just glared at him. He was much too joyful about all of this for her liking. *Of course, he's thin and athletic, so he's not worried in the least about fitting through whatever tight places lay ahead.* Realizing that her heart was pounding, she wiped her sweaty hands on her skirt and tried to calm herself down.

"How long will it take to get inside Cam−... the fortress?" Marcy asked, taking a deep breath.

"It will be dusk by the time we exit the tunnel on the other end," Ulnick answered impatiently, "if we ever get started. Are you ready?"

JoJo, Marcy and Trip all nodded. The Gnome leader didn't hesitate to see if someone came up with a last-minute question. Turning on his barefoot heel, he disappeared into the darkness of the tunnel, followed by the next two Gnomes. Ulnick had already sent a couple of his soldiers ahead to guard against any surprises.

"What did he say about 'others' using these tunnels?" Marcy asked as they made their way forward.

"Nothing to worry about, Marcy," JoJo clucked her tongue at her friend, ducking into the entrance. Marcy hesitated, earning her a gentle nudge from behind from Trip.

"C'mon Marcy, you can do this, no problem," he offered encouragingly. She bent forward holding the glow-rock in front of her and took the first couple of steps into the cave. Just as she started to feel a little bit of relief, she heard Trip add, "Just remember to watch out for the tunnel creatures!"

Chapter Twenty-eight

Stumped

"Ouch!" Marcy yelped, just a couple of steps in front of him. *That's* got *to set some kind of record*, Trip thought to himself. *No one can hurt themselves that many times.* He didn't think she'd taken five consecutive steps without hitting some part of her body on the edges of the tunnel. It'd be different if she didn't have a glowing rock in her hand to at least show her what to avoid.

"You alright back there, Marcy?" JoJo asked somewhat over her shoulder, afraid to turn her head too much or she would bump into something painful, also. Marcy mumbled something back that was between words and a whimper that JoJo took as a sign that she was okay, in the barest sense of the word. "Ulnick just passed word back that we're almost there."

They had been making their way through the narrow, winding tunnels for a couple of hours. On a handful of occasions, they had come to complete stops while the soldier Gnomes

dispatched of snarling, unseen creatures who happened to be sharing

the underground maze with them right then. JoJo preferred not to

know what these things were, but Marcy had asked nonetheless, the

knowledge somehow more soothing to her. One of the nearby

Gnomes explained that the sounds were most likely coming from

giant weasels who had come to think of the tunnels as their home,

despite their having done nothing more than squat here to justify

their claim.

A couple of times, JoJo had felt something on the tops of her

feet and, looking down, had discovered large centipedes crawling

across her shoes. On each occasion, she had stomped her feet to get

rid of the creepy six-inch long creatures, making her bump her head

painfully on the low ceiling. Instead of *Ouch!* something much

worse spilled out of her mouth. It would undoubtedly have earned

her a sprinkle of red pepper on her tongue if her Dad had been

around.

The biggest problem for JoJo and her friends had been the

tiny size of the tunnels. More specifically, the price to be paid every time they had to squeeze through tight, sharp gaps. By the time this was over, they were sure to have more scrapes and cuts all over their bodies than they'd ever experienced before. There had been one instance that Trip had been convinced would be the end of their journey. JoJo had – with a great deal of difficulty and no small amount of bad language – managed to work herself through a tight space. Marcy wasn't even going to try, having completely assured herself that she didn't have a prayer of getting through that gap after just having watched her much more athletic, thin and nimble friend struggle to do the same. A special Gnome was summoned forward, and he managed to chip enough rock away with his pick-axe to enlarge the passageway slightly. Marcy still cut herself in a couple of different places, and screeched and wailed under her breath all along the way, but in the end was able to pull herself through the opening and back up to her feet on the other side. She then watched Trip negotiate the same tight space in about three seconds, seemingly without picking up so much as a scratch.

"We are here," Ulnick announced from up ahead.

JoJo and the others looked up and noticed for the first time that they were in a much wider section of the tunnel, almost like a room. Even the ceiling was high enough that she and her friends didn't have to worry about their heads. On the other side of Ulnick was an actual door. It was small by human standards, but large enough for the twelve-year olds to crawl through on their hands and knees. It had not yet been opened.

"Before we go up, we should decide *where* it is that we desire to go," the Gnome leader stated. "I have no intention of wandering aimlessly among the Black Wind and other scum on the surface. It is time to consult your map." He was looking straight at Marcy, who complied by removing the scroll from the inside of her vest and unrolled it onto the stone floor.

The map was a very detailed rendering of the layout for Camelot, almost a blueprint of sorts. Buildings were easy enough to make out, and tiny descriptive text labeled some of the less obvious structures, such as the stables and storage rooms. On the side of the parchment was the more recently-added cryptic writing that hopefully told them where to find the *Chrimeus*.

E	L	X	H	U
J	D	R	T	B
A	P	V	Y	N
M	S	I	Q	F
G	O	C	W	K

E	T	O	N	E
H	S	D	R	H
T	U	C	R	N
O	E	T	N	V
E	E	E	T	S

"What do you make of this?" an elderly Gnome asked another of seemingly equal age. They had spilled out of the tunnel with all the others, and had taken a position right in front of the map, opposite of Marcy. "I mean the map is genuine enough, but what of these boxes of letters?"

"I'm not sure," the other replied, bending low to get a better look, although he was already pretty close even when standing straight up. "At first, I thought it might be some strange tongue, but the letters appear to be straightforward enough. Apparently, they are coded in such a way as to conceal their true meaning. Let's see if we can make any sense of this."

Evidently, these were the scholar-Gnomes that they'd been told about. Marcy thought that she'd finally found someone among the community of little people that she could identify with, but they seemed content to tackle the challenge without her. After all, these guys had hangnails that were older than she was.

Ulnick paced impatiently back and forth while the academic Gnomes mumbled ideas to one another. JoJo poked her head into the mix once or twice to see if anything about the puzzle jumped out at her. Trip never even gave it a glance, figuring that he was way out of his league if this riddle was stumping the Einsteins. He spent the time checking out the various outfits of the Gnomes, comparing the weapons that the soldiers wielded to some of the tools carried by others. After a while, both he and JoJo ran out of things to look at.

"Well?" Ulnick finally demanded after he decided that he could wait no longer. "What have you found?"

"Patience, young warrior," one of the scholars replied. "Are you afraid that the fortress will no longer be there if we take a bit longer?" Marcy stifled a chuckle.

"How much is a 'bit longer'?" Ulnick shot back, clearly agitated by the elderly Gnome's teasing tone. "This day will be over soon. When it is, according to these humans, the witches will seize another child for their evil experiments. So I ask you again: how much longer?"

"We are not able to decipher this," the other academic sighed. "At least, not without the benefit of more time and possibly other resources."

JoJo's mouth hung open in shocked disappointment. "What are you saying? That we came all this way for nothing? Let's go on up there and start looking everywhere. We can't just give up, for crying out loud!"

"I'm afraid that is not –" Ulnick started to say, but was cut off.

"It's a sequential substitution code," Marcy said flatly. "The grid on the left is the sequence. If you notice, there are no duplicate letters and no Z. So, it's a map to tell you how to read the one on the right. When you do that, you get 'The seventh stone under Ector.'"

Everyone in the tunnel chamber stared in silence at her. The scholars looked back and forth between the two collections of boxed letters to confirm what she said, nodding their heads after a brief moment.

"You surpass us," one of them admitted to her, admiringly. "I don't know what length of time we would have required to arrive at this solution."

"Did you just now figure this out?" JoJo asked, a combination of awe and suspicion in her voice. Marcy's sheepish facial expression answered the question. JoJo's tone turned sharper, "How long have you known?"

"I had a pretty good idea of how to determine the answer right away, back at your house," Marcy said, more embarrassed than proud. "I kept pulling the puzzle out to work on it whenever we stopped. Finally, the whole thing clicked while we were waiting for you to get up that morning at Maude's. I didn't say anything because I was afraid that the only reason you brought me along was to eventually solve this. If I gave you the answer early, you wouldn't have any more need for me. Lord knows, there have been plenty of places along the way that you would've been tempted to dump me, and I can't say I blame you. I didn't want to get left out, no matter how much you guys think I can't do this stuff."

Surprisingly, it was Trip who responded. "Geez Marcy, for a smart person you sure do think dumb sometimes. We're a *team*, you know? Not everyone on a team has the same strengths, but a good team uses the right people in the right situations. Without you, we'd have a huge hole in our team."

Wow, she thought. *Seriously? Did Trip Dowling just call me his* teammate? Her head was spinning.

"So, Goofball," JoJo interrupted Marcy's reverie, "do you have any idea what 'The seventh stone under Ector' means?"

"That much I can answer," the first Gnome scholar answered when Marcy hesitated. "Your search will take place in King Arthur's ancient Meeting Hall of the Round Table, or what's left of it. I cannot imagine how anything was hidden in that ruin."

Chapter Twenty-nine

Sir Ector

Sir Ector, the wise Gnomes had explained, was one of the original Knights of the Round Table. Furthermore, he had actually been foster-father to Arthur while the future king served as a squire in the older man's court, at the request of Merlin. Ector had, in fact, been a king in his own right, ruling over a small realm in the southwest part of the country. There were conflicting stories about whether Ector had been kind to Arthur prior to the young legend's ascension to the throne. Some histories had shown the older king to be cruel to the squire while favoring his natural son, Kay. Whatever the case, Arthur had bestowed seats at his Round Table to each of these men as a show of his trust and gratitude.

"That's all great," JoJo said when they seemed to have come to the end of the story. "But what's the seventh stone under him all about?"

Once their destination had been determined, Ulnick produced a strange-looking key and unlocked the small door. In single file, they passed through the doorway – JoJo, Marcy, and Trip on hands and knees – and proceeded down a very small tunnel. After about fifteen minutes of crawling, JoJo and her friends were able to stand up again as they reached another chamber-like room. By the light of their glow-rocks they could see several dark openings leading off in different directions. Ulnick again confirmed with the scholars that they wanted to go to the former gathering place of King Arthur and his Knights, and then led everyone through one of the doorways. Luckily, it didn't require anyone to crawl on their hands and knees.

"Each Knight had his designated place at the Round Table," one of the scholars finally answered, "with none of the seats placed more highly than any other, including Arthur's. My sense is that we need to find where Sir Ector's chair was located and from there we should be able to find this seventh stone."

"So, you don't really know then?" JoJo challenged excitedly. "How the heck are we supposed to find where this Ector guy sat? Is there a nametag or something on the table?"

"Calm down JoJo," Marcy urged in a softer voice. There were also loud whispers of "Shhh!" coming from ahead of them in Ulnick's direction. "Let's wait until we get up there and take a look at the room. There might be something there that helps us out."

They all felt the change in slope as the tunnel started to angle upwards. At first, it was slight and didn't require much more effort than before. That quickly changed when it got steeper in a very short period. JoJo leaned forward into the hill as they climbed, using her hands on the ground in front of her for balance and support. She thought she could feel a warm breeze from up ahead. Up until now, there had not been the slightest stirring of air, and the temperature of the tunnels had been mostly cool and dank.

The tunnel leveled out again, at the same time that its ceiling became much lower, forcing JoJo back to her hands and knees. Up ahead, she could see dusky light filtering through a small opening, silhouetting the heads of the Gnomes. After a few minutes, she crawled through the tiny entranceway into one of the greatest legendary rooms of all time – the Meeting Hall of the Round Table.

"Whoa! How neat is *this*?" Trip said as he followed Marcy through the wee doorway and climbed to his feet, brushing the dirt from his knees. "Check this out!"

JoJo and Marcy were already doing just that. The first thing that struck them about the hall was its sheer size. It was enormous, easily larger than the gymnasium at their school, and it was crowned by a high vaulted ceiling. Great blocks of granite made up the single massive wall, which continued all the way around the circular chamber. Tall windows stretched high above the floor, allowing the last light of day to provide a slight bit of grayish illumination.

As large and majestic as the once-proud hall had been, it was now equally run-down and sad. The remains of what were once a pair of humongous wooden doors dangled limply on their hinges, the wood mostly shattered and the iron twisted and rotting with rust. Very little stained glass was still attached to the windows, and what was there were mostly broken shards protruding at unsightly angles. All of the great wooden shields that had hung proudly around the entirety of the round wall and identified the finest knights in the land now lay in heaps on the floor, smashed beyond recognition into ugly splinters. And there was the table.

"Oh my God!" Marcy exclaimed, one hand partially covering her mouth. "Is that really it? *The* Round Table?"

In the center of the huge chamber sat the remnants of the most legendary table in history. The gigantic oaken piece of furniture had easily been forty feet across, and made of thick planks of one of the hardest trees known to man. That had not been enough to keep it from being utterly destroyed by Camelot's conquerors. With a force that only Pewtris Grimm himself could have commanded, the Round Table had been cleaved, as if by a monumental axe wielded by a vicious giant. Rather than having it dismantled and removed, Grimm had left the crumpled table as it was – a reminder of a defeated kingdom and their smashed dreams.

"It's so… sad-looking," JoJo said after taking in the enormity of the scene. "I guess anyone who could destroy *this* had to have been pretty powerful. That's what we're up against."

"Yeah, well if he's all that big and bad, why is he so worried about a *Marble?*" Trip asked. "You know, I saw where we used to feel that way about the Russian hockey team a long time ago. That they were just so much better than anything we could hope to put on the ice, and then a bunch of American college kids ended up beating them in the Olympics."

"First of all, they were the 'Soviet Union' back then," Marcy corrected with a grin, "and secondly, what does that have to do with *this?*" She swept her empty hand to take in everything in the room.

Trip was more than a little shocked that she'd known what he was referring to, but quickly shook that off. "Easy. This Pewtris Grimm guy is not the superman that everyone makes him out to be. He's got weaknesses just like that supposedly unbeatable hockey team did. For one thing, we know that he's afraid of whatever someone with the *Chrimeus* can do." With that, he winked at JoJo.

"Well, let's start looking," JoJo agreed, throwing her hands up in the air. "Do we have any idea where our Sir Ector's chair would have been?"

All of the chairs had been long since smashed into little more than firewood, the cushions rotted and the padded armrests eaten away by rats and other vermin. On top of that, it would have been difficult to say which chair had gone to which spot on the table, given that there were no telltale differences in the surviving splinters. JoJo and her friends turned to the two academic Gnomes for further guidance.

Ulnick was also anxious to get on with the search. He had dispatched soldiers to various points around the great chamber, acting as both lookouts and their first line of defense, should that be necessary. He had also sent a scout party out to attempt to locate JoJo's father.

JoJo, Marcy and Trip weren't really sure what they should be looking for, so they watched the scholars and tried to mimic them. The problem was, the wise Gnomes seemed a bit lost, too. They directed a few of what looked to be miner Gnomes to start poking around the floor with their pick-axes. To JoJo, it looked like they were randomly digging, hoping that they'd miraculously hit the right spot.

"Sir Ector would have been seated right in this area, if the old texts are correct," one of the scholars said. JoJo couldn't tell one from the other, and had given up trying to do so. "So it stands to reason that the seventh stone under him would be somewhere nearby."

"I don't think that's it," Marcy said, thinking out loud. The scholar Gnomes and everyone stopped what they were doing, and stared at her, waiting. She looked from the general area that they were prying around up to the wall behind. "Where would Sir Ector's shield have hung?"

The two scholars looked at one another for the answer, but with the same result. Nothing. "What are your thoughts?" one of them asked.

"I believe that if we knew where on the wall his shield usually was, we would use that to count down seven of these stones, and *that's* where we'd find what we're looking for."

JoJo and Trip exchanged glances, as if they were evaluating what Marcy had just said. Both shrugged their shoulders and made the same *How-the-heck-do-I-know?* faces at the same time. "Sounds good to me," JoJo pronounced, looking at the Gnomes.

"She's brilliant," one of them said admiringly, looking to the other for confirmation. Both nodded their heads at Marcy, who was now starting to get slightly red-faced at all the attention. Turning to the other Gnomes, the first scholar ordered, "Search through the wreckage of the shields. We're looking for three green oak trees on a field of white."

The Gnomes scattered to the piles of splintered and smashed shields lying in piles all around the great hall. Often, there was barely enough of a shield remaining to determine what the crest on it had been. They found bits of red lions, gold dragons, and blue falcons. Black stripes and solid oranges. JoJo picked through the debris right alongside Marcy and Trip, searching for...

"I've got it!" a Gnome from across the chamber shouted. Everyone stopped what they were doing and ran over to him. Sure enough, he was holding a shard of wood upon which was painted part of a green tree on a white background.

Marcy looked up at the wall directly above them. The outline from where the shield had hung prior to the meeting hall's destruction was dimly visible. From the bottom tip of the silhouette she counted down seven of the wall's huge stones. Standing confidently in front of everyone, she reached up and touched one.

"Right here," she said. "This is our stone – the seventh one under Ector."

Chapter Thirty

A Handful of Trouble

The sight was as funny as could be had in the ruined Meeting Hall of the Round Table. Trip and JoJo stood apart, holding opposite ends of a rough flat piece of wood that had many centuries earlier been part of one of the great doors leading into the chamber. This particular piece was only three feet long and no wider than either of their heads, which is about how high they were balancing it. Perched on the small plank were three Gnomes flailing away with pick-axes at the stone in front of them.

"Marcy, are you sure this is it?" JoJo asked anxiously. "Because I'd hate to think my arms are getting tired for nothing."

"Seventh stone under Ector," Marcy answered without taking her eyes off of the block of granite. Pointing at the lower right-hand corner of the stone she asked the nearest Gnome, "Take a look at that corner by your foot. It looks like there might be something there."

He and his companions stopped beating at the rock. Bending low, he peered closely at a slightly discolored section where she had pointed. The Gnome scraped at the corner with the sharp tip of his pick and found a small hole between stones. He wedged the point of his tool into the opening as far as it would go, and then pushed on the handle. Surprisingly, the huge stone rotated, pivoting out toward the Gnome on this end while moving inward on the other end.

"Look! Down at this end" Trip shouted for attention. Like JoJo, he was tired of holding the Gnomes up on the board, but the excitement of the stone moving had reenergized him. Everyone looked to see what he was talking about. "Something just fell from the top of the hole when you guys made the rock move in on this end."

A dark velvet pouch sat just inside the lip of the opening. The nearest Gnome moved to retrieve it.

"Halt!" shouted one of the scholars. "That should not be touched by any of the Pure Folk, if it is indeed one of the Five Marbles. Move back and let the humans be the ones to handle it."

JoJo and Trip gladly lowered the short plank to the floor, the Gnomes just as glad to be back on firmer footing. Marcy and Trip looked at JoJo, and the unspoken message from both of them was clear. *This is your show. Go ahead and do it!*

She rubbed her hands together before reaching up into the opening. Her fingers found the pouch and closed around it, the velvet oddly smooth in the midst of all this stone. Pulling her hand down, she held the object of their long search in her palm, concealed only by the pouch. She looked again at her friends, as if for encouragement. Neither was the least bit patient at the moment, having experienced pretty much the same trials she had to get to this point.

"What's the matter?" Trip asked. "You having second thoughts or something?"

"No… heck, no!" JoJo responded a little more strongly than she'd intended. "I just don't want to – you know – mess it up." Looking down at the pouch she continued, "Okay, let's see what we've got here."

Marcy and Trip seemed to be holding their breath as their friend loosened the tie around one end of the small dark velvet bag. Flickering light spilled out of the slightly opened end, as if a lit match were within. JoJo looked inside before sticking her hand in, holding the open end up to her eye. She saw what she was looking for, or at least what she thought she was supposed to be looking for. Reaching in, she extracted a small glass ball the size of a walnut from out of the pouch. Holding it between her thumb, index and middle fingers, the *Chrimeus* threw off a warm luminescence that was brighter than a mere glow but not so much as to be blinding.

"Geez, that's it JoJo!" Marcy exclaimed, hopping up and down excitedly, which was completely out of character for the biggest geek of Mahoney Middle School. "You are the owner of something I would have denied even *existed* a couple of days ago. I don't know exactly what it's supposed to do, but I believe it when they say it's especially powerful."

"I just wish I knew what to do now," JoJo answered, still staring at the flickering Marble.

"You can start by taking that and getting as far from this place as possible," a deep voice replied from across the great room. It was somewhat familiar. The gloomy fading light inside the meeting hall made it difficult to make out details, but the profile of this man was enough for their recognition. Caleb.

"Where the heck have you been?" Trip asked before JoJo had a chance. "I thought you were supposed to meet up with us."

"Yes, that is true," the Free Knight answered, walking toward them. "I said that I would meet you at the gates of Camelot. Only you didn't go to the gates, did you?" He was now close enough for them to see one of his eyebrows arched high on his forehead.

"Did you *really* expect us to just go up to the front door of this place and knock?" Marcy laughed incredulously. "I mean, the Black Wind have been chasing us practically ever since we left you. Whatever orders the Gories gave them, it must have included maximum harassment. I nearly drowned at one point!"

Caleb grimaced at her ranting as he came to a stop a few feet in front of them. The soldier Gnomes appeared to be comfortable in his presence, making it fairly obvious that they'd had dealings with

the Free Knight as an ally of the Pure Folk on prior occasions.

Ulnick seemed especially pleased to see Caleb.

"In case you forgot, I'm not going anywhere without my

Dad," JoJo said, sticking her chin out at the older man for emphasis.

Shaking the *Chrimeus* at him, she added, "One way or another, I

plan on using this thing to free my father."

"I cannot allow you to turn the *Chrimeus* over to Pewtris

Grimm, either directly or through his demon-spawn daughters. I

assume that you also have not forgotten this. Unfortunately or not, it

appears that you have bound the Marble to you, so it cannot be taken

from you without your consent."

"What do you mean by 'bound'?" Marcy asked, always

trying to figure things out. "All she did was pull the *Chrimeus* out of

its little pouch. It's not like she said some magic words or smeared

her blood all over it."

Caleb scratched his head in bewilderment. "Are you

certain?" he asked, directing his question first at Marcy before swinging to face JoJo. "The 'little pouch', as you call it, is actually an enchanted carrying vessel for the *Chrimeus*, fashioned by Merlin himself. The idea was that no one would be able to accidentally open it and either expose the Marble or become bound to it. It requires some knowledge of magic to merely open the container."

Everyone looked at JoJo, including the Gnomes. She had stopped waving the *Chrimeus* around, although its internal light continued to flicker in the creeping dusk.

"What?" she said to all of her companions at the same time. "What's everyone looking at? You guys all saw me – I didn't do anything. The pouch just opened when… I can't even do a card trick, for Pete's sake!"

Caleb looked at the scholars, who both shook their heads from side to side, signifying that the girl did or said nothing unusual that they were aware of.

"All right then," the Free Knight said after a moment of deep thought. "I guess the challenge is for us to get out of here with both the *Chrimeus* and your father."

"I'd also like to free those little children that the Gories have been kidnapping in my name, if you don't mind," JoJo added, looking him in the eye.

"Would you like to bring back King Arthur while we're at it?" Caleb asked in exasperation, no smile on his face to go with the sarcasm. He furrowed his brow, considering all of the different aspects of what they were trying to accomplish. "I sure could use Beglis in this situation, even if he doesn't share our zeal about all things. His magical ability could prove useful against the witches."

The mention of the warlock's name sent a shiver down JoJo's spine. *I've still got* that *to deal with when this is all over*, she reminded herself. *If we make it that far.*

"Why didn't you just bring him along with you?" Trip asked.

"I didn't have time to go back for him. After I arranged for him to meet you three at the rock in the forest, I had a great deal to do before arriving here, and it was no small distance, even on horseback. I trust your rendezvous with him went as planned, given those counterfeit LifeStones dangling from your ears?"

JoJo shuffled uncomfortably. "Yeah, we met him all right. But you forgot to tell us that we were going to have to pay for his services."

"Pay?" Caleb was clearly taken aback. "Beglis certainly has his peculiarities, but he would never extract payment for something like this. He despises those ear manacles as much as anyone, and would gladly rid the entire kingdom of them for no more than a 'thank you'. What exactly did he require as payment?"

If JoJo was unsettled before, it was nothing compared to how she felt now. She held the *Chrimeus* up in front of her. "This."

Instead of reacting in shock and anger, Caleb nodded his head knowingly. "Tell me, what did Beglis *look* like?"

"What do you mean?" Trip asked, annoyed by the question. "You know the guy better than us. Fancy suit. A little bald on the top. Kind of a grandfather-like face. When he wasn't being a – what did he call it? – Glutton."

The Free Knight's face darkened and he faced JoJo squarely.

"Beglis is big and robust with a wild mop of rusty hair. He looks more like the village drunk and has never worn anything but dingy robes in all the years I've known him. The one to whom you promised the *Chrimeus* is none other than Pewtris Grimm himself!"

Chapter Thirty-one

A Song and a Dance

JoJo stared at Caleb with her mouth wide open, but no words came out.

"You know," Trip interjected, "you could've told us what he looked like *before* we went to meet him. I mean, you sure did spend a lot of time describing the big rock and the arched trees and all that stuff."

"What does it mean?" Marcy asked, trying to ignore Trip. "The fact that JoJo promised the *Chrimeus* to… um, you-know-who?"

"Oh for Pete's sake, Marcy! You can say *his* name, you know? It's 'Camelot' you're not supposed to say out loud, although that doesn't seem to matter anymore, either." JoJo had snapped out of her temporary paralysis with a sudden need to lash out, even if it was at one of her best friends in the world. Turning to Caleb, she asked, "So what? I told Pewtris Grimm that he could have the *Chrimeus* if he got rid of those nasty earrings. It's not like we're dealing with the most honest guy in the world, are we? What happens if I don't give it to him?"

The Free Knight rubbed his chin thoughtfully before answering. She could tell that he was having trouble trying to organize his response. When he was ready, he lowered his hand and spoke.

"That is the dilemma, isn't it?" he asked, but it was definitely more of a statement than a question. "On the one hand, you must fulfill the contract that you made with Grimm, and provide him with the *Chrimeus*. Also, without conceding the Marble, you cannot free your father, who is also my dear friend and brother-in-arms. On the other hand, however, neither I nor the Gnomes will stand by silently and allow you to place such power in the possession of the one being in the entire world who is intent on destroying us. Neither choice allows for victory, only different degrees of defeat."

Trip pointed his finger accusingly at Caleb. "This isn't *your* choice to make. It's not mine or Marcy's, either. And not the Gnomes. Only JoJo gets to decide. Me and Marcy came here because she's our friend, and we're going to stick with her, no matter which way she chooses."

Caleb regarded the boy with an almost amused look, as did Ulnick. There was no doubt among them that the Free Knight could easily take the young hockey player across his knee in an instant, if he were so inclined. There was also little question as to the loyalty of JoJo's two best friends, no matter their other differences. While Caleb admired the spirit of the three children, he was also frustrated by their predicament. Before he could say another word, however, there was a commotion at the main entrance of the meeting hall. Along with the others, he peered into the gloomy half-light in that direction. And froze.

Standing in front of the broken doors was a pair of Half-locks accompanied by a dozen Black Wind foot-soldiers. Worse yet, when JoJo and her companions looked around the chamber, they were astonished to find each of the smaller exits also guarded by black-cloaked Assassins. Gnomes had been placed to warn against such visitors, but it was apparent that the tiny sentries must have been dispatched in one way or another, without having uttered the least sound of alarm.

"I think we can help you with your conundrum," one of the Half-locks said hoarsely from across the huge room. The familiarly raspy voice carried as if he were standing ten feet in front of them. He extended a long bony finger at JoJo. "Bring the little bauble here, and I will relieve you of all your troubled indecision."

JoJo looked around, trying to gage the situation in the growing darkness of the chamber. *It would be so much easier if I could just* see! she thought to herself in frustration. The entire Meeting Hall of the Round Table erupted into bright light at that very instant, blinding everyone to one degree or another. JoJo's eyes seemed to adjust to the illumination faster than anyone else's as she wondered, *Did I just do that?*

While everyone's vision was correcting for the sudden change in light, JoJo decided to try to answer her own question. She focused on the two Half-locks, considering them to be the biggest threat at the moment. *Have you guys ever slow-danced together?* The *Chrimeus* glowed a little more brightly in her hand. Trip and Marcy burst out laughing.

With their arms wrapped around each other and their heads lovingly resting on one another's shoulder, the two usually-dreaded sorcerer-servants of the witches moved together in a small circle just inside the main entrance. JoJo smiled at the sight before realizing that something was missing. In the next breath, Assassins from all around the chamber were singing an appropriately slow-moving romantic song. When her friends recognized the tune as something popular from back home, they broke out in laughter all over again.

Caleb and Ulnick were more awestruck than amused. The same with the scholar Gnomes, for they all knew what they were witnessing. For the first time since Merlin walked the halls of Camelot a thousand years earlier, someone was wielding the ancient power of the *Chrimeus*. That it was a twelve-year old girl from a strange world was all the more wondrous. Not to mention, she had turned two of the most feared creatures in all the kingdom into dancing puppets, and two dozen vicious warriors into an all-boys chorus.

"Are you enjoying yourself?" Caleb asked her with one eyebrow raised high. Despite his gruff tone, he was inwardly pleased that he hadn't been required to deal with the Black Wind. Even with the *Chrimeus* located, the Gories and Pewtris Grimm would continue to exterminate any Free Knights they located. His walking right into Shadowrock was about the same as a surrender, at least in their eyes. Caleb's intentions, on the other hand, in no way included the idea of giving himself up.

JoJo turned her attention back to the slow-dancing Half-locks. Holding the Marble firmly, she gave her arm a whirl. Instantly, all of the Black Wind Assassins in the room crumpled into heaps on the floor. The Half-locks stopped waltzing and turned to face her, holding hands like middle-schoolers out on a date.

"Take us to see the Gories," she commanded in a voice that was steadier than she felt. "Now!"

She began walking across the meeting hall, her path curving to match the wall and the outer rim of the broken Round Table. Marcy and Trip were on either side of her, both anxious to ask the first question. Before either of them had a chance to say anything, she turned back to Caleb, Ulnick, and the rest of the Gnomes.

"You guys don't have to come. I know it's wicked dangerous for you to be around all these people, and your being there isn't going to make me decide one way or the other about what I need to do. So, I really appreciate everything you've done, but why don't you head on back now? My Dad ought to be able to tell us how to get home from here." She waited for them to do as she suggested, but deep inside she knew that that was not going to happen.

Ulnick was the first to speak. "My lady, I know that we have but just met, and that under the direst of circumstances, but know this: Gnomes are the last of the Pure Folk to exist in any numbers to speak of. The Leprechauns, Fairies, Fast Turtles, and other beings that count themselves among the Pure have all seen their numbers dwindle to almost nothing. Some do not even trust others *among* the

Folk, much less those that would openly do us harm. Many of my men have already perished on this mission, given the appearance of the Black Wind scum where I had posted sentries. I will not dishonor them nor my king by retreating in the face of known peril. You shall not part with us so easily."

'My lady' and not 'girl'? I guess manners change quickly when you start whipping magic stuff around, JoJo mused silently. After letting the rest of what he'd said sink in, she felt really bad about the perished Gnomes he'd mentioned. *But are they doing this to help me and Dad, or to keep me from handing the* Chrimeus *over?*

"I believe I have already pledged my sword and my life to you once," Caleb followed after he was certain that Ulnick was done. "Nothing has transpired that would have me retract my oath."

JoJo looked them both over. "Okay, but I hope neither of you plan to do anything stupid to keep me from getting my Dad back." She then spun around and resumed her march toward the main doorway, her eyes focused straight ahead as she concentrated on the task ahead.

"Do you already know what you're going to do?" Trip whispered out of the side of his mouth as he kept pace with her. When she didn't respond, he pointed ahead and added, "I don't care how mad you might get at me some day, you better not *ever* make me do something as stupid as what you're doing to those dudes."

JoJo shot him a half-smile.

"What does it feel like, JoJo?" Marcy asked, amazed at everything she'd just witnessed in the past couple of minutes. "I mean, can you feel some kind of magical power flowing through your body?"

"Not really," JoJo mumbled as they continued to follow the hand-holding Half-locks through the former grand entrance and out into the abandoned courtyard. A couple of Gnomes lay motionless on the ground, some of Ulnick's sentries who hadn't had a chance to warn them of the Black Wind's coming. JoJo's stomach tightened at the sight. *These are my fault.*

They continued across the courtyard, the darkness pushed aside by the magical illumination *desired* by JoJo. Led by the enchanted Half-locks, they entered the castle proper, passing guards who seemed to not care one bit about the intruders. *I hope it's this easy with the witches*, she thought as they passed into what was once the great throne room of Camelot, where in better times sat the legendary King Arthur and his magnificent queen, Guinevere.

Today, perched on disgustingly mangled thrones sat the current ruler's daughters: Creech, Vomus, and Muisance – collectively known as the Gories. They hissed at the performance put on by the enchanted Half-locks, who were now directly in front of the witches and had resumed their dance. Raising an ugly hand, Creech released a blast that eliminated the Half-locks altogether, disintegrating them into little more than gray dust. She then faced JoJo.

"I believe you have something for us." It was not a question.

Chapter Thirty-two

A Strange Audience

For the first time since entering the throne room, JoJo noticed the Half-locks lined up along the walls. There had to be at least fifty of the evil-warped magicians in the chamber. The two that had just been disintegrated were apparently not going to be missed, she mused as she considered what they were up against. She needed something better than dancing warlocks or this would turn out to be very ugly.

On either side of her stood her two rock-solid best buddies – Trip the stud hockey player, and Marcy the brilliant dweeb. A few steps behind them stood the Free Knight who claimed to be her Dad's best friend. At his side was the grizzled leader of the Gnome expedition, Ulnick. The two scholar Gnomes were the only other ones in their party who had entered the throne room, Ulnick directing the others to remain outside but vigilant.

"I want to see my Dad before this goes any further," JoJo said when she was done surveying the insides of the huge chamber. It may have once been splendid during Arthur's time, but the place now gave off an incredible sense of... dreariness. She clenched the Marble tightly, making sure that no one was going to take it from her easily.

"All in due time," the oldest Gorie – Vomus – replied. "I would like to know exactly *how* you gained access to the magic of the *Chrimeus*. You hardly seem capable of much more than a few tricks. Even that old crackpot Merlin could do better than that." She cackled, and her sisters joined her in the forced dry laughter. It was sickening to watch, mostly because the witches didn't appear to know how to laugh.

"I'm glad you're getting your jollies," JoJo snapped, pointing the *Chrimeus* threateningly at all three. "But I don't really care what you *want*. You guys don't really even matter, do you? Only your father really counts. Even if I were to hand the Marble over to you, he'd just end up taking it for himself. Isn't that right?"

The Gories were plainly outraged, but silent. JoJo had no desire to hear what they had to say, so she continued before any of them had a chance.

"Bring my Dad out here now, or so help me..." She tried to look as threatening as possible, but part of her was afraid that she looked no scarier than a pouty little kid. *I've got to see what else I can do with this Marble or we're going to be in big trouble*, she worried quietly while trying to remember to keep a stern outward face. *On the other hand, I can't screw it up or they'll figure out that I don't really know what I'm doing.*

Her threat seemed to have a slight effect on the witches, or at least on Muisance, who mumbled something to her older sister before speaking aloud. "Fetch the prisoner! Once we have Daddy up here to watch, I think it would be a fitting lesson to teach you your place in the world, *Chrimeus* or no." She pointed a hideously crooked finger at JoJo.

"I don't like this," Trip murmured softly with his hand casually covering his mouth. "What's the plan, JoJo?"

"That makes two of us," Marcy whispered, but without taking the extra precaution of concealing her speech. Leaning forward to see around JoJo, Trip shot her an incredulous look. Too late, Marcy's hand went up to her face, stiff and obvious as she added, "Sorry."

The Gories stared menacingly at the three middle-schoolers, perplexed by their behavior and trying to determine what they were plotting behind their little hands. Before they could say anything, their attention was diverted to one side of the massive room. A large wooden cage on wheels was being pushed through one of the many side entrances and into the center of the chamber, such that it was about the same distance from both the witch-sisters on the elevated dais and JoJo and her companions. Slumped inside the cage was a half-clothed man whose body bore the marks of a skilled torturer's handiwork.

It took JoJo a moment to recognize her own father. It took her another moment and two tries before any words would come out of her mouth.

"Dad!" Her eyes watered at the sight of the strongest man in her world, apparently beaten almost to death. At the sound of her voice, he started to move his head in JoJo's direction, but the attempt was too much for him, and he collapsed in a heap. One hand clenched a cross-bar of the cage, but that was his only sign of life. Tears rolled freely down her cheeks in a steady stream. *Oh, Dad! What did they do to you?*

"Not quite so perky now, eh little girl?" Creech snickered from her perch. "It's such a shame that he doesn't seem interested in what's going to happen to his sweet Magoo."

JoJo jerked her head sharply in the witch's direction, horror plainly painted on her face. *How…? Not even my best friends know about that!*

"What's the matter, cat got your tongue?" Creech cackled sickly. "Oh, we know a great deal more about you than your father's pathetic little nicknames, girl. Do you seriously think that this was the first time we've stepped into your wretched excuse of a world? We have known for a while where to find that cowardly Free Knight runaway, having followed him all those years ago when he thought he was escaping in secrecy."

"My Dad is *not* a coward," JoJo said through gritted teeth.

"Your father isn't *brave* enough to be a coward," Muisance talked over her. "You should have heard him whimpering like a young girl before we even got really started with him. He…"

"*Shut up!*" JoJo screamed, spit flying from her lips. Her entire face was flushed a bright red as she squeezed her eyes tightly shut.

She didn't see one of the scholar Gnomes tug on Marcy's skirt. Thankfully, neither did any of the Gories. Marcy looked down curiously, but managed to do so without drawing attention. She mouthed the word *What?* but felt like she had to look back up in the direction of the witches before she got her answer. Another tug. In a very controlled manner, Marcy glanced down without moving her head. Her eyebrows came together, indicating that she didn't think this was a good time for a chat. A series of tugs now, even while she was looking at the scholar.

What in the world? Marcy pressed her lips tightly together to keep from blurting her annoyance out at the Gnome. Then it hit her. Some of the tugs were shorter and some were longer. *He's sending me a message… in Morse code!* She returned her outward gaze to the Gories on the dais, but her focus was on the dots and dashes being transmitted via her skirt.

Calm. Her. Down. Marcy thought about the message, figuring that 'her' referred to JoJo. She waited for more, but there was nothing else. *Calm her down. What's that all about? Are they worried about JoJo making a scene or something? Seriously?* She looked around the throne room without moving her head too obviously. And gulped hard. While all the commotion surrounding JoJo and Mr. Mallory had been going on, the Half-locks had slowly started moving away from the outer walls, gradually tightening the noose around all of them. *Now I get it!*

"JoJo, take it easy," she said softly out of the side of her mouth. "They're trying to get you all worked up because it keeps you from using the *Chrimeus.* You have to shake it off. Now! The Half-locks are closing in on us!"

Trip made no attempt at being inconspicuous as he whipped his head all around to verify what Marcy had just said. It had broken his heart to see and hear what the Gories had been doing to his best friend, but now he understood. He'd never known a hockey player who truly played better when angry, and that's what they'd done to JoJo. He turned to face her, putting his hands on her shoulders.

"Hey Kiddo, do like Marcy says. Real quick-like, too. They've been playing you like a cheap set of drums. We need you to forget all the stuff they said. That was just to get inside your head so that you wouldn't be able to concentrate on doing your magic thing. Come on, take a deep breath and get rid of all the junk."

The Half-locks had now formed a semi-circle around the group, the ends butting up against the throne dais. They were no more than fifteen feet away when they came to a stop. Through bleary eyes, JoJo could see that each of the corrupted warlocks carried a wooden stave about the length of a sword. On the top-end of each stave was circle about the size of a grapefruit made out of some kind of rough iron. Within the circles, dark blue-and-orange threads of lightning crackled. In unison, the Half-locks all lifted their staves and pointed the circles toward JoJo and her companions.

She quickly wiped her eyes and gave a big sniff, signaling that she was done feeling sorry for herself. With the *Chrimeus* firmly in her grasp, she reached inside herself and directed the Marble's power. Everyone – including the Gories – watched in awe at the outcome.

The lightning within the iron circles changed to a solid white light, no longer flickering, as the staves were raised straight up into the air with the Half-locks unable to release them. Soon, all fifty Half-locks were lifted off the throne room floor to a height that was almost half-way to the high vaulted ceiling. The iron circles seemed to have taken on a life of their own, as they now all pointed to the center, connecting to one another and making one large circle of suspended Half-locks. Without warning, the circle descended directly over the witches, the brightness of the white lights joining together to form a dazzling brilliance that no one could look at directly. And then it winked out, leaving the massive room in complete darkness.

JoJo summoned light from her Marble, just enough to illuminate the room without blinding anyone.

On the throne dais sat… nothing. Not a throne. Not a Half-lock. Not a Gorie.

Nothing.

Chapter Thirty-three

Pewtris Grimm

"Holy mackerel, JoJo!" Marcy exclaimed after what seemed like an eternity of no one saying anything. "What did you do to them?"

JoJo didn't answer. In all her life, she'd seldom felt greater satisfaction than she did right now. If some Greater Power decided that what she'd done was wrong, then so be it. *You don't mess with my family. Period.*

She looked at the bestial cage that held her father. The guards had run like rats as soon as the Half-locks had started floating overhead. The beaten body inside the cage barely resembled the man that was the dearest to her in all the world. Any world. She broke into a run, worried that they might be too late.

Caleb was a half-step behind her, with Trip and Marcy close on his heels. The cage door was held shut with a simple clasp, fastened from the outside. There was no lock, probably because the prisoner was not very likely to try to escape. JoJo pulled the door open and... stopped. She had no idea of what to do next. His shirtless body was covered with bruises and deep slashes, and she wasn't even sure how to touch him without causing more pain. Not to mention, her Dad was much too heavy for her to try to lift, even under the best of circumstances, which these definitely did not qualify as.

"Please, let me do this," Caleb offered, gently easing her out of the way. "He's still breathing, but not much more than that. There's no telling what's broken."

He reached under his fellow Free Knight and very carefully eased him across the floor of the cage to the doorway, where he motioned for Trip to help with the legs. Together they managed to tenderly lay him on the stone floor. His breathing was shallow, and he winced in pain without opening his eyes.

"What do we do?" Marcy asked, feeling more helpless than ever. "He needs full-blown medical care, and we don't even have a first aid kit."

"If you would allow us to take a look," one of the scholar Gnomes interrupted. It was the same one that had tugged Marcy's skirt earlier. He and the other scholar moved closer to JoJo's Dad, each moving to different parts of the body. "We have more than a little experience with trauma." His inspection appeared to focus more on the chest and abdomen, especially the heart and lung functions, while the other Gnome concentrated on the head, peeking under eyelids and looking into the mouth. After a short while, they both stopped their prodding and looking and listening.

"His physical torture stopped a while ago," the same scholar announced. "Many bones are broken, but his organs all seem to be intact and working well enough. His mind, however, is not... how do I say – free?"

"What's that mean?" JoJo asked in a small voice, her heart sinking. "Is he going to be okay?"

The other scholar cleared his throat before answering. "Your father has a darkness inside of him. It was put there to hasten his torture when mere physical means did not suffice. This darkness has wrapped itself around his mind, causing him the worst kind of despair. I'm afraid that many of his wounds were those he inflicted *himself*. He would rather end his life than continue as he is."

"So, how do you fix it?" Trip asked for JoJo, who was struggling to wrap her head around what had been said. "I mean, you guys are wicked smart. So is Marcy here. Between all of you, I'm absolutely *positive* that you can come up with a way to make him better, right?"

JoJo looked hopefully at the tiny scholars. In response, they bowed their heads rather than return her look. She turned to Caleb, but was met with the same sad silence. Kneeling down next to her Dad, she began to weep again.

"Perhaps I can help," a familiar voice announced. "In fact, I *know* I can help. It's more a matter of how badly you would like my assistance."

JoJo and her companions all turned their heads in the direction of the voice. He was standing in the shadows to one side of the throne dais. Abruptly, he leapt up gracefully onto the elevated platform where the mangled thrones had sat minutes earlier, along with their occupants. In that elegant, brown pin-striped suit, one could never guess that he measured his age in centuries, if he measured it at all. He stepped into the light so they could see him better. And bowed.

"Beglis!" Marcy gasped.

"That is not Beglis," Caleb growled. "As I explained before, you were tricked. Beglis is a much handsomer creature than this."

"Hah!" the man on the dais shot back, pointing a shiny, lacquered walking stick at Caleb. "Jape all you wish, Free Knight. Methinks your days are numbered. And very *low* numbers at that."

"Hold on a minute!" Trip intervened, looking at Caleb while pointing at the man. "Didn't you say that this is Pewtris Grimm?"

"There you go!" the man responded, waving his stick in a flourish. "I just *knew* that you were not half as dense as you appeared back in the woods. And look! – you even brought cute little hole-diggers with you. I probably should have had those 'secret' passages filled in long ago, but it's been so entertaining watching you tip-toe in and out of the castle, thinking that you were being so clever. As a fellow king, I guess the neighborly thing to do would be to invite Odnil over to discuss it... before I stuff them full of Gnome children."

"You're pretty sick..." Trip started to say, but that was as far as he got.

Everyone in the throne room was suddenly frozen in place, as if blast-chilled in a super-efficient deep freezer. Everyone, that is, except for Pewtris Grimm and JoJo. She looked at her friends, and then stood up to face him, the *Chrimeus* glowing brilliantly.

"Well, well, I guess you know –" Grimm began.

"Shut up." She didn't yell it, but it came out with more venom than a thousand vipers could have mustered. "You can't have it. I've seen some of what it can do, and I've only scratched the surface. I can't even imagine someone as purely disturbed as you are with this kind of power. It's bad enough what you can do already, but that part's not my fault. I'm not going to add to it."

"Tsk, tsk, tsk." He pointed the walking stick at her as he spoke. "I don't think you know this game very well at all. You see, that darkness infecting your father's mind right now will stay forever, if I don't get the *Chrimeus*. Let me assure you that he would rather die a thousand times each day. Not to mention, you've already promised the Marble to me in exchange for earlier services, if I recall correctly."

JoJo fought the urge to get angry, remembering what had happened with the Gories. Without being too obvious about it, she drew a deep breath and blew it slowly back out through her nostrils. Rolling the *Chrimeus* in her hand, she looked at Marcy and Trip, Caleb, Ulnick and the scholars. *I can't do this by myself,* she admitted to herself, wondering at the same time if Grimm could read her mind. She gripped the Marble tighter and willed her friends out of their suspended animation. Pewtris Grimm showed just the slightest trace of worry on his well-groomed face.

"Could you guys hear okay while you were frozen stiff?" JoJo asked all of them, but no one in particular. "I just don't want to repeat anything if you already heard it."

"We understood all that was said well enough," Caleb answered for everyone, "although it was as though the sounds were being transmitted under water. How did you...?"

"That is unimportant," Grimm interrupted, waving a hand dismissively. "Whether you listen is not significant. Perhaps it is better that you witness everything, after all. It seems that the young lady has difficulty retaining the details of her bargains."

"Stick a sock in it, Grimm," JoJo said, her mind made up about how she was going to proceed. "I made a deal with Beglis, not you, so get over it. Also, I've decided that you can't have either my Dad or the *Chrimeus*. You need to get rid of that poison that you stuck in his head."

"Well now, that is not exactly what I would call a negotiation," Grimm replied smugly. "You see, you have left out the part where you offer something in return for the demands on my generosity. Otherwise, you are wasting my time."

JoJo bit her lip involuntarily. The last thing she wanted to do right now was to show uncertainty. She needed Pewtris Grimm to think that she knew more about using the magical power of the *Chrimeus* than she really did. She also needed to hang onto the Marble long enough to understand better how it worked. What she truly required right at this instant was for Grimm to buy what she was selling.

"I'll bring you two of the other Five Marbles."

He hesitated only slightly before responding. "I shall require all four. And your father as a hostage."

"No deal. Dad goes home with me, *without* the evil stuff in his head. Three Marbles."

"I will be your hostage," Caleb interjected. His tone was not one of defeat, but rather honor. "Let me replace my friend."

JoJo considered what the Free Knight had just offered. He was willing to put himself through a million agonies that no one could possibly imagine, for the man she knew only as her Dad. She met Caleb's gaze, and could see that he would not be denied. A tear ran down her cheek.

"Three Marbles and a Free Knight," Grimm smiled. "It appears we have a deal."

Chapter Thirty-four

No Looking Back

JoJo opened her eyes and tried to figure out where she was. Nothing in the room looked familiar as she struggled to get her bearings. *What the heck happened?* she demanded of herself. She pushed herself up to so that she was sitting and could get a better look at her surroundings.

The first thing she noticed was the peacefully sleeping man next to her. Dad. It had been a bit of a challenge getting him loaded into the softly-cushioned carriage that they'd been able to locate on the grounds of Shadowrock. One of the castle guards said that it had belonged to the Gories, but that was no longer a concern with the witches gone. Pewtris Grimm had done as promised, and lifted the dark veil that had been imprisoning Kevin Mallory's mind. The physical healing would take much less time now that his free will had returned. Unfortunately, the same could not be said for Caleb.

The last that she had seen of the Free Knight was the sad vision of him walking away with Grimm. There was no cage involved, which probably made the entire scene even more heart-wrenching. It would have been easier to accept had the evil sorcerer forcibly locked him away. Thankfully, Caleb did not look back at JoJo and her friends. He simply walked with hunched shoulders, resignedly following Pewtris Grimm back into the shadows of the fortress. *I'm coming back for you*, she swore under her breath. *I promise.*

"Did you sleep okay?" She was stunned to discover that the voice belonged to her Dad. "I've been afraid to move for the past couple of hours because I was worried about waking you."

JoJo stared at her father. It wasn't the first that he'd spoken – that had taken place in the carriage ride – but she still felt like it had been ages since she'd last seen him. Not to mention, there was a lot to catch up on from *before* all this started to happen. She felt like they would have plenty of time for that, now that they were safely back together.

"How long was I out?" she smiled at him.

He smiled back. "A while, but you needed it. We all did."
He grimaced as he moved to a sitting position.

Most of his broken bones and cuts had been mended by a
combination of the Gnome healers and his own daughter's newly-
acquired magic, but the process was by no means complete.
Additionally, it would take a good amount of time before the
specters that haunted his mind were forever silenced, if ever. He
would never wish that on anyone… His face betrayed his thoughts
as he wrestled with what they'd told him about Caleb taking his
place.

They had stopped at the home of the Gnomes, gaining access
to the vast mountain through the heavily-guarded supply entrance.
Generally, humans and others were not admitted beyond the
doorway, but these were no ordinary visitors. Ulnick had cleared the
way for their prompt and gracious reception, before heading off to
report to King Odnil. That was two days ago.

"We need to get going," JoJo said after a while. "I feel like every day is an eternity to poor Caleb, so the sooner we can find those other Marbles, the sooner we can get him back." She looked sadly at her father, knowing what he was thinking. "Dad, I didn't have a choice. Caleb volunteered without warning me or anything, and Grimm just said 'yes' before anyone knew what was going on."

"I know. I've been told by your friends what happened." He reached over and put his arms around her. She wanted to hold him tightly, but remembered the tenderness of his wounds and gently laid her arms on either side of him, burying her face in his shoulder. JoJo had never been one to show weakness in any situation, preferring to put on a brave or carefree face no matter how fouled-up things got. But this was different. In seconds, she was crying heavily into her Dad's comforting warmth, her small body heaving with the uncontrolled release of emotion. Patting her lovingly on the back, he said, "Magoo, you did great. No one else in the world could have pulled that off. You're not responsible for the choices other people make. Caleb knows that I would have done the same for him. That's what makes us Free Knights."

She pushed herself away a little more forcefully than she intended, and wiped her eyes with both hands. Staring at her father, she asked, "When – if *ever* – were you going to tell us about that? I mean, the whole Free Knight stuff and all? Did Mom know?"

He pressed his lips together for a moment before answering. "I… I tried to explain it to her once. She didn't handle it too well, to say the least." His stared at his daughter and blew out a steady stream of air before continuing. "That was the day she jumped off the bridge. After that, I was real scared to say anything to anyone, especially you and your sisters."

"I don't get it," JoJo's face softened. "Why would that make her want to commit suicide?"

"It was too much of a shock for her, and she claimed that our whole marriage had been based on a lie," Kevin answered, pushing his hand through his hair. "She said she didn't know what to believe any more, and that none of this was fair to her or you and your sisters. Then she left."

JoJo sat motionless and silent, her twelve-year old brain trying to process what she'd just heard. For some reason, she'd been able to accept that she could travel to a whole new world through a secret passageway in her basement, but the thought of her own mother jumping into the freezing waters of Casco Bay over something like this was baffling.

"What about the clues you left behind?" she asked, finally breaking the silence. "Who were those for?"

Her Dad hesitated again, thinking about how to word his answer. "They were for the 'right' person, whoever that turned out to be. I was always hoping that I could one day pass on my responsibilities to one of you girls, but I wasn't sure how to go about it."

"That's why you told us those bedtime stories, wasn't it?" JoJo's face brightened suddenly. "Because you wanted us to know something about the history of this place. I thought some of these things sounded familiar as we were whipping through the kingdom!"

Kevin smiled gently. "That was part of it, the mental part. I struggled with the physical part. It wasn't like I could take you out into the yard and start training you on how to become a Free Knight. And there had never been a female among our number before."

"So, you were disappointed that you never had a son? That one of us wasn't a boy?" The accusation in her voice was clear.

Her Dad chuckled. "No, I can't ever say that. Believe me, there's nothing that a boy could've done better than you. For that matter, there's not a grown man or woman in the history of Erristan who has ever stood toe-to-toe with the Gories before, much less defeat them so thoroughly. JoJo, you've accomplished more than all the Free Knights who have ever lived put together. But even if you hadn't, I wouldn't trade you for anyone. The same goes for your sisters."

"Even Ronnie?"

"Even Ronnie," he grinned.

The smile returned to JoJo's face, which was now a tear-stained mess. Along with her sleep-rumpled hair, she was quite a sight. "Speaking of my sisters, you know they're going to be wicked put-out with me and you, right? Like this was some kind of special vacation that they didn't get invited on, or something stupid like that. Never mind the fact that Marcy and Trip and I almost got killed on more than one occasion. And not to mention what *you* went through, for crying out loud."

"Well, I think that explaining everything to Maggie, Ronnie and Scrap will be a walk in the park after these past few days." His smile betrayed a weariness that said how much he'd really endured. It was more than the sheer tiredness of his ordeal, however. There was an occasional haunted look in his eyes that told her that the demons were not completely gone. Not by a long shot.

"I think they'll be okay once you get to the part where they have a *grandmother* who'd love to meet them," she said, trying her best to pull him away from memories of his nightmares. "All you gotta figure out is whether Maude goes back to Ferry Village with us, or the girls want to come here for Spring Break."

He didn't answer right away, and his best attempts to maintain his smile were giving out. "Magoo, there's something I need to tell you." She tensed suddenly, the tone of the conversation having changed dramatically with that one little sentence. *Now what?* "I won't be going back home right away. Not with you and your friends, anyway. I can't. Not while Caleb is being tortured in my place."

JoJo was flabbergasted. The silence caused by this shocking news seemed to last forever as she tried to process the implications of what her father just said. A thousand questions competed in her head for the right to come out of her mouth.

"But, what do I tell the others? You know, Maggie and Ronnie and Scrap?" she finally asked, unable to come up with anything more important. "You know that they're not going to believe a word about any of this if it's only coming from me and my friends."

She watched her Dad's face as he struggled with whatever answer he was thinking about. His lips stayed pressed together, as if to prevent the wrong response from leaking out of his mouth.

Finally, he put his hands softly on her cheeks, the way he always did

whenever he had something extra-special to tell her.

"Josephine," he said, using the name he reserved for serious

occasions, "you are the most powerful wizard since at least Merlin,

and possibly even more so than him. You have sworn on my best

friend's life to find these other Marbles, and every day that you

delay is a lifetime of agony for him. You have dealt with witches

and sorcerers – I have every faith that you will come up with an

acceptable way of explaining things to your sisters."

Chapter Thirty-five

The King's Road

They finally bid farewell to King Odnil, Ulnick and the other Gnomes the following day. JoJo and her friends were sufficiently rested, and her Dad was deemed fit for travel. Loaded into the same carriage that they'd taken from Camelot, they headed along the river on the King's Road, back to the town of Bettafly. Back to Maude.

Marcy had had the most difficulty with leaving the mountain because of the amount of time she'd spent with the scholars. There was no amount of knowledge that they possessed that she wasn't willing to sit and soak up. The reverse was also true. The Gnomes had never heard of many of the technological advances that were commonplace in the twelve-year old's world. It had been especially amazing to her that the concepts of refrigeration and electrical distribution were of more interest to them than cell phones or tablet computers. Of course, Marcy had been all too happy to both describe the history of their development and explain how they worked.

Trip had taken to playing the Gnomes' favorite game, which was like nothing he'd even seen before. Of course, it took place inside the mountain, and involved a great deal of running and – for him – ducking. He had come to think of it as playing multi-ball soccer on an obstacle course made up of tunnels. The balls were made from the bladders of some animal that he couldn't remember, and were about as big as baseballs. Their size made it easy for the Gnomes to kick around, but much harder for Trip. Not to mention, many of the tunnels required that he watch the ceiling rather than the ball. He left the mountain with cuts and scrapes all over his crew-cut head.

"I sure wouldn't mind another ride on the Fast Turtles," Trip said wistfully, watching the Crystalline River through one of the windows as the carriage ambled steadily along the packed-dirt road. "That was my favorite part of this whole… whatever."

"I thought my grandmother's stew was your favorite," JoJo challenged.

"And you were just raving about that suicidal game you played non-stop with the Gnomes," Marcy added.

"Okay, okay," he said, holding up his hands. "All I'm saying is the Turtles are pretty cool, and I'd do that again in a heartbeat."

Marcy and JoJo followed his gaze toward the river. "I wonder whatever happened to Vili and Yama. I mean, we never got to say anything to them after we split up in the mountain."

"The Estrilli will be there when you need them," Mr. Mallory answered, surprising them. "As long as your intentions are for the good of the land. Those water-elves have a way of being able to tell the good guys from the bad."

The journey to Bettafly turned out to be uneventful. Occasionally, they would pass travelers headed in the other direction, some on foot but most either on horseback or in wagons. They did not see a carriage anywhere near as nice as their own. Nor did they see the loathsome LifeStones dangling from anyone's ears any more. Apparently, the ugly earrings had been tied directly to the Gories, and had fallen away with their downfall. The inhabitants of the kingdom were still trying to figure out whether that was a good thing or bad. Additionally, the nursemaids who cared for the kidnapped children at Shadowrock had sworn that the babies disappeared into thin air at about the same time that the Gories had been defeated. JoJo hoped that that meant the small kids were reunited with their families, but she'd have to figure out a way to confirm it.

Nowhere to be seen were the Black Wind. Those mercenaries had been the enforcers for the witches, another relic of the past with no place in the kingdom. Pewtris Grimm had not taken an active role in the governing of his kingdom, having left that to his three wicked daughters. Perhaps he would find a role for the Black Wind as he realigned his administration. Then again, he might usher in an entirely new line-up to enforce his rule. For the time being, the people of Erristan had a break from the smothering presence of imperial thugs.

The guards at the gate recognized the carriage, if not its passengers. Pretty much everyone in the kingdom knew the unmistakable shape and colors of what had always announced the arrival of at least one of the Gories. Not that the witches required such a conveyance to travel from one place to another, but it made for proper intimidation. There was an expected hush as the driver pulled the carriage to a stop in front of the entrance. The gates were wide open, giving nearby townsfolk a good view of the new arrival. Most of the people had either frozen where they were, or scurried down the various side alleys to get as far away as possible.

"Hallo, there!" the driver shouted cheerfully. The guards, who had been trying to figure out what was going on, stared open-mouthed. No driver of this particular carriage had ever said anything in a cheerful manner before. Ever. "We would like to enter your fair town. With your permission, of course."

The guards looked at one another, mouthing the words, '*With your permission?*' Finally, the sergeant-in-charge stepped forward, careful to maintain his bearing for fear of offending whoever was riding inside. He was like anyone else in the kingdom, in that he was still trying to determine what to make of the world ever since his LifeStone suddenly and unexpectedly fell away days earlier.

"Who should we have the honor of welcoming?" the sergeant asked politely, taking extra caution to ensure that his tone matched his words. The last thing he wanted was for one of the witch-sisters to burst through the door and turn him into some ghastly creature.

Indeed, one door slowly opened. While everyone watching held their breath, the guard sergeant gulped, worried that he'd just spoken his last words as a human being. Out stepped a young girl with a wild mop of auburn hair. Most unexpected of all was her huge, warm smile.

"Hey, fellas!" JoJo waved casually to the guards. "We're just here to visit my grandmother. No big deal. I hope that's okay with everyone." The shock on the faces of the guards and the townspeople could not have been any greater if she had just stepped off of an alien spacecraft. She pointed at the carriage while continuing to face her awestruck audience. "Look folks, the Gories are *gone*. History. Kaput. They're not ever coming back. Same with their Black Wind hooligans. So you don't need to keep walking around on pins and needles."

"What about... um, you know?" one of the guards asked. He looked sheepishly from JoJo to the sergeant, whose quizzical expression said he wasn't sure what the question was. But JoJo knew.

"Pewtris Grimm is, unfortunately, still around," she responded. "Maybe someday, we won't have to say that anymore, either. But seriously, he doesn't really care a whole lot about you guys. He's after something... different."

She decided not to say anything about how bad things would get if Grimm acquired that 'something different'. These people deserved whatever short break they could catch, after centuries of being bullied every minute of their lives. It was time to give misery a little rest.

There was an unseen commotion growing back among the crowd of gathered townsfolk. As people moved out of the way, an opening formed to allow the source of the noise to come forward.

Bobbing energetically through the vacated space was a stout, gray-haired woman.

"Maude!"

Chapter Thirty-six

Middle School Blues... Again

JoJo, Marcy and Trip sat at a table in the cafeteria of Mahoney Middle School. Marcy picked at her yogurt cup while JoJo sipped water from a plastic bottle and surveyed the huge room. Trip played uncharacteristically with his ham and cheese sandwich, paying no attention to the other students who stared at the unlikely trio.

"So, what's next?" Trip asked, surprising the girls.

"What do you mean?" Marcy asked in return. "I thought you had your hockey to do."

Trip rolled his eyes at JoJo. "You don't 'do' hockey. It's something you play. If you're any good. Anyway, I don't think I'm going to fall too far behind if we... you know?"

Along with Marcy, he looked at JoJo.

"What?" she asked, throwing her hands up at her sides.

When they didn't back off, she added, "Okay, okay. I'm trying to

figure it out. But I don't want either of you to feel like you're

obligated or anything."

"Seriously?" Marcy replied a little too loudly, prompting

JoJo and Trip to motion with their hands for her to keep her voice

down. She continued in a hoarse whisper. "Do you honestly think

you can do this *without* us? How were you planning to find the

next... you-know-what... on your own? For Pete's sake, JoJo, just

because you're the most powerful wizard to ever come out of Ferry

Village!"

JoJo and Trip chuckled, causing Marcy to break into a smile.

She couldn't help but sneak a peek at the other kids in the cafeteria.

Never in her wildest dreams had Marcella DiPietro ever envisioned

herself sitting at the coolest table at Mahoney, the envy of all those

classmates who'd called her mean names behind her back for so

long. No matter how hard she tried, she still couldn't make herself

look like this was normal. *Give it time*, she told herself. *You're not

used to being smart* and *cool*.

JoJo knew she was right. If it wasn't for Marcy, she wouldn't know the first thing about any of the other Marbles. While she had been spending all her energy making sure that her Dad was going to be able to recover from Pewtris Grimm's torture, her brainiac best friend had gathered so much information from the scholar Gnomes. But not everything.

She also knew that there was no way that Trip was going to let her go off on another adventure and not take him along. They'd been practically joined at the hip since they were born, and she was very aware that he would always have her back. No matter what. Just like when they got back home.

Their return had not been without incident. Her Dad had directed them to the necessary return portal, the same one he had used to land in Ferry Village decades earlier. When they climbed the stairs back up to the Mallory basement, they'd only been able to open the secret door because of JoJo's newfound magical abilities. Once inside and up to the first floor, they had been assailed by the other three Mallory girls. It took more than a few minutes to get everyone calmed down enough to tell the story.

JoJo had decided that her sisters deserved the truth. Well, most of it, anyway. She kept her intentions to herself, sharing those only with Marcy and Trip. Maggie, Ronnie and Scrap had taken some convincing, of course. JoJo actually had to turn Ronnie's feet into a pair of flounders before they started to believe her. Luckily, she was able to reverse the feet-fish magic trick. Of course, they all wanted JoJo to produce things for them: Maggie wanted a car, Ronnie strongly suggested money, and Scrap asked for a boat. More than anything else, though, her sisters all wanted to know when their Dad was coming home and when they'd get a chance to meet their grandmother, whom JoJo had been forced to describe over and over, especially to her little sister. She chose not to say anything about the conversation she'd had about their mother, figuring that was Dad's responsibility.

Marcy, of course, had a heck of a time trying to explain to her mother where she'd been for several days, why she hadn't called, and what happened to her cell phone. Somehow, she'd convinced her mother that while they were camping and fishing with Mr. Mallory, she'd dropped her cell phone through the hole in the ice because she'd gotten so excited about actually catching a fish. By the time she got done also making up stories to account for her newly-acquired scrapes and bruises, she felt absolutely terrible. She vowed she'd come clean with her mother once they were completely done saving mankind from Pewtris Grimm and whomever else posed a threat to the planet.

For Trip, his absence has been noted more around the local hockey ponds than at home. His mother had trusted that he was in good hands at the Mallory house, and she'd been too exhausted from work to go chase him down. The fact that his skates and hockey stick were in JoJo's living room had told the other Mallory girls that he was wherever their goofy sister was. He'd wasted no time heading straight to the nearest rink for some serious ice time.

"So, are you going to help us with our homework again?" Trip asked Marcy, grinning. "But next time, you've gotta dumb it down a little so that the teachers know it's mine."

JoJo chuckled, while Marcy was trying to figure out if he was kidding or serious.

"Okay, there are four more Marbles, right? How do we know which one to go look for next?" JoJo looked from one of her best friends to the other. "Or where, for that matter?"

"Perhaps I can help," a familiar voice offered. The three sixth-graders looked all around, failing to see the source. "In here."

JoJo almost threw her water bottle. Peering at them from inside the plastic cylinder was the smaller – but unmistakable – form of their favorite Leprechaun.

"Flick!" JoJo nearly shouted, causing a group of nearby eighth-grade girls to look their way. She tried to cover most of the bottle with her hands. "What are you *doing* in there?"

"That's pretty gross," Trip laughed despite JoJo's scowl. "I wonder how long he's been sitting in there." He winced as she punched his arm.

Flick somehow seemed to float inside the bottle as if it were the most natural place in the world – any world – for him. He smiled as he looked from one friend to the next. "Name which Marble you seek next."

Marcy was the only one of the three who knew the names. *Aquiium. Bixas. Jouzze. Vamilloux.* She didn't know what differentiated one from the other, if anything. Even the scholars had had limited knowledge of much more than the sketchiest of legends. Since JoJo had promised to deliver three of the four, she decided that it didn't much matter which one they started with.

"*Aquiium,*" Marcy said for no special reason that she could think of, other than it was first alphabetically. And she was nothing if not logically organized.

"Fine," the Leprechaun replied, smiling still.

"What's that supposed to mean?" JoJo demanded, trying unsuccessfully to keep her voice down. A table of seventh-grade boys was now openly staring at them. She gritted her teeth at them until they looked away. Returning to Flick, she asked, "Where do we find this *Aquiium?*"

"In the lost city under the seas, of course," he answered. "Atlantis."

Acknowledgments

So much goes into writing a children's adventure novel. More critical than the ability to spin a good story or craft a well-turned phrase is the need to stick with it and see one's efforts through to the end. That doesn't usually happen without the emotional support of a core group of true believers. For me, that group consisted primarily of Amanda and Chris, Christine and Pete, Christie, Samantha, Marie, Wes, Gretchen, and – of course – Vicki. They put up with this process for the past six years, and for that I am eternally grateful.

I would also like to thank those who helped out with beta-reading one rendition or another of this story – Jeff, Theresa, Sophie, Eric, Erin, Stephen, Sara, Ed, Priscille, and Stacey (God, I hope I didn't leave anyone out!).

Lastly, I want to say how thankful I am that I had an opportunity to grow up – at least, for a little while – in Ferry Village. You'd be hard-pressed to find another place like it.

About the Author

Steve Peaslee went to ten different schools spanning three countries during his childhood as an Army brat. Of course, Mahoney Middle School – then known as Mahoney Junior High School – was one of those. He eventually ended up at the US Military Academy at West Point, where he graduated as the second-most punished member of his class. His Army career included a tour as a paratrooper in Italy, another as an artilleryman in Colorado, two different courses at the Defense Language Institute, and a Master's degree at Harvard. Steve's civilian life has been a lot more boring, mainly spent as an investment advisor in Louisiana.

Steve has four daughters whose birthplaces mark his career – Italy, California, Japan, and Louisiana – and who served as the inspirations for his writing (but not the models for his characters!). He lives with his wife, Vicki, who *also* has four daughters. There's a story in there somewhere!